# GUY NOIR AND THE STRAIGHT SKINNY

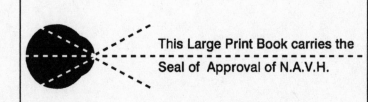

This Large Print Book carries the
Seal of Approval of N.A.V.H.

# GUY NOIR AND THE STRAIGHT SKINNY

## GARRISON KEILLOR

**THORNDIKE PRESS**
*A part of Gale, Cengage Learning*

GALE
CENGAGE Learning®

Detroit • New York • San Francisco • New Haven, Conn • Waterville, Maine • London

**LIBRARY OF CONGRESS CATALOGING-IN-PUBLICATION DATA**

Keillor, Garrison.
    Guy Noir and the straight skinny / by Garrison Keillor.
        pages ; cm. — (Thorndike Press large print basic)
    ISBN 978-1-4104-4812-5 (hardcover) — ISBN 1-4104-4812-6 (hardcover)
    1. Saint Paul (Minn.)—Fiction. 2. Large type books. I. Title.
    PS3561.E3755G89 2012b
    813'.54—dc23                                                                2012010232

Published in 2012 by arrangement with Penguin Books, a member of Penguin Group (USA) Inc.

Printed in the United States of America
1 2 3 4 5 6 7 16 15 14 13 12

To the memory of Tom Keith (1944–2011), who did gunfire, squealing tires, the pigeons on the windowsill, the dripping faucet, the footsteps in the alley, the sirens, the voice at the other end of the line, the dogs, a squeaky chair, glass breakage, the beer tap and martini shaker, an occasional French waiter, a growly incomprehensible gangster named Biggie, and much more. An ex-Marine sergeant, star centerfielder, and amiable golfer, he was the son of radio performers and worked on "A Prairie Home Companion" from its inception in the summer of 1974.

# 1
# TAKING A MEETING
# WITH MR. ROAST BEEF

Call me a cynic, but I maintain that nothing can clarify a man's thinking quite like looking down the barrel of a revolver in the hand of a man who is irked with you and considering homicide as a solution to his problems. This has happened to me from time to time in my so-called career as a private eye in St. Paul, Minnesota, and each occurrence promoted clear thinking, inconvenient though it was at the time. Christians try to find clarity through prayer, but you don't really know what prayer is until you meet someone who's prepared to shoot you. I am thinking in particular of an afternoon last February when an eighty-two-year-old gorilla named Joey Roast Beef sat quivering in my office on the twelfth floor of the Acme Building with a cocked pistol aimed at my chest and ordered me to tell him something that I had no intention of telling him because it involved the beautiful prospect of vast wealth I was in no mood to share. His hairy finger was coaxing the trigger and he yelled, "Talk to me!" and suddenly everything got clearer, The Delicate Beauty of Life and its Fragility and The Sudden Relative Insignificance of Constitutional Law and the Dow-Jones Average.

Moments before, on this particular February day, on the twelfth-floor, high above the poor souls struggling through the crotch-high snowbanks along Latimer Street, all was well, no inkling of imminent peril. I was savoring page fourteen of a trashy novel in which a twenty-three-year-old fashion model is attracted to a heavyset sixty-four-year-old galoot in a wrinkled blue suit and the two of them are sharing chicken quesadillas and his knee is pressed firmly to her thigh and she does not seem to mind. I was thinking about ordering a chicken sandwich from Danny's Deli and hoping Danny would add it to my tab, though my tab was long, two or three hundred bucks, which is not good, but business had been slow and a guy's got to eat. Chicken on a kaiser, slice of onion, and a squort of hearty mustard to clear the sinuses. My long underwear had gotten bunched up in a way that made me think about my prostate, and I was thinking about that, and the sandwich, and the fashion model ("her thigh was firm but pliable, even, he hoped, complaisant"), while listening to a voice mail from Doris, my landlady at the Shropshire Arms, saying she's sick and tired of me being two months late on the rent, and the honeyed voice of my ex-love Sugar saying she's sorry but she can't have lunch with me on my birthday in March (*Sixty-five!!! Moi??? The poor man's Philip Marlowe? Yikes!!!!*) because she and Wally are taking a Caribbean cruise — so I'm in a Dark State of Mind when I hear heavy thumping on the door, and the thumper yells, "Hey, Noir, open up. I know you're in there, ya duckbutt." And it was him, the Senior Citizen of Organized Crime.

"The office is closed, Joey," I said in a calm, businesslike tone of voice.

"Not to me it ain't." And he threw open the door and stomped in, all 340 pounds of him. "Forgot to lock your door, Noir. What a genius. It's amazing someone didn't rub you out a long time ago."

He was draped in a blue seersucker suit, like a toad in gift wrap, and a yellow shirt and pink tie, his thinning black hair slicked back, peering out through thick black horn-rims, and he looked like one of those fat generalissimos with a chestful of medals who run banana republics, though the jacket lapels had traces of schmutz on them, but his beetle brow was set for battle, his jaw jutting out, his dewlaps quivering, he was wheezing — as you or I would if we were five feet four and weighed 340 pounds and carried an oxygen tank with a plastic tube stuck up our nose.

"No 'Good morning'?" I said. "No 'How are you'?"

"I know how you are. You are in big, big trouble, smart guy. I'm done with you. If you don't tell me what I need to know, you're gonna be swimming in the river in a pair of concrete shoes." He lowered himself gingerly into my old oak chair, which groaned under him, pulled out his Colt .45, and aimed it at my sternum. It appeared to be loaded. With bullets. Real ones.

"I'm expecting visitors, Joey," I said in the same calm tone. "Lieutenant McCafferty and Captain Calhoon. Our weekly hand of whist. So I don't have time for an extended visit."

It was a lie, of course, but when dealing with an angry, armed man, you'd like him to think that witnesses could arrive at any moment.

"This won't take long. About two minutes. The word on the street, Noir, is that you

10

are holding out on me on a very lucrative deal involving millions — and you made a big, big mistake thinking I'm such a ditz I wouldn't get wind of it, which is a grave insult. I am not the type of person who accepts being insulted. And I'm gonna give you about two minutes to tell me what is the deal and when do I get my split," he said. "So out with it. Sing. Let's hear it."

"Give me a hint," I said. "I got no idea what you're talking about. You want to know who to pick in the seventh at Belmont? You want the formula of the hydrogen bomb? Warren Buffett's cell phone number? What you want, Joey?"

"It involves you and that hootchie-kootchie dancer at the Kit Kat Klub named Naomi Fallopian. The one who got her Ph.D. and now she's teaching women's rights or something at the U. So let's start with her." He shifted his enormity in the chair, and it groaned, and I could imagine it collapsing and him sprawled on the floor, a mountain of adipose tissue, and me leaping up and whacking him senseless with the desk lamp. I could also imagine the shock of the fall twitching his trigger finger and a poof of flame and the bullet hitting me in the frontal lobe and turning me into a human cauliflower. The second possibility

11

seemed more likely.

He cleared his throat. "This dame and you. You two are walking around about to make a killing and sashay off to a penthouse somewhere with a revolving king-size bed under a silver ceiling mirror with her in her pink peignoir reflected in it, and that's okay, I don't begrudge you the comforts of life, I'm only looking to collect my share, otherwise Miss Fallopian is gonna be wearing a black suit and a hat with a veil and crying into a hanky as she gazes at the china vase containing your ashes." He set the pistol down on the desk and adjusted his air hose, which was taped to his upper lip.

I said, "Joey, I respect your perspicacity in most things, but as to this scuttlebutt somebody sold you about me and Miss Fallopian, Joey, you are woofing down the wrong rainbow, there is no pot of gold at the end, just an old private eye with lower back pain and a pocketful of breath mints, namely me. There is no killing about to be made. Whoever whispered this in your ear is pulling your leg. I say this as an old and dear friend. This is delusional thinking, Joey. If you're not careful, you're going to wind up on the funny farm, talking to the window shades."

I was hoping to build doubt in the man's

mind, but his firm grip on the peashooter indicated otherwise. He was in no mood for Story Hour. "Tell me what's going on, Noir, or else you are gonna get you a new buttonhole. Right in between those other buttonholes."

It occurred to me that prison might not be a great deterrent to a man of eighty-two. By that time, a person has had all the freedom he knows what to do with. He has squeezed that orange. There is no more juice in it. A small cell might come as a comfort to him.

"If I were you, I would go home and ask the beautiful Adele to fix you a mai tai or two and then lie down and take a nice nap. You're obviously under a lot of stress right now. You don't want to get yourself a coronary."

"You're gonna be under even more stress when this bullet hits your rib cage," he said. "The last man who double-crossed me is wearing the pine kimono, Mister. He's taking the dirt nap. If you get my drift. Start talking, or I'm gonna roll the credits." And then he cocked the pistol.

That little metallic skritch and click clarified my thinking but good. *I am not going to beg for my life, precious as it may be, especially with Naomi Fallopian involved in it,* I

13

thought. *I am not going to crawl. Au contraire. I will keep on pushing Joey's buttons and rile him up so he goes nuts and maybe shoots himself in the kneecap.*

"Listen, fat man. You ever hang out up around 102nd and Broadway?" I says. "That's where I grew up. New York, New York, the city so nice they named it twice. We used to use guys like you for footrests. You're darned right I have hit pay dirt, and it's mine, lard ass, no freeloaders. Your mooching days are done. You can wave your hardware all you like, I am not going to let a schtoonk with an air hose and pee-stained pants to help himself to the gravy." I said it quiet, but I said it straight.

He was mightily peeved. "The clock is running out, buddy boy. You take this wiseacre attitude with me, and I will mash you like a grape." He stamped his foot so hard, the tassel came off his shoe, and the exertion squeezed his hemorrhoids and he let out a yelp.

"You really ought to see a proctologist," I said. "They can snip those hemmies off with a pair of pinking shears and cauterize them with a curling iron, and it'll probably improve your love life and add twenty points to your bowling score."

He shifted the pistol from his left hand to

14

his right, and his tone changed. He started pleading. "You and me go way back, Guy. I have been like an uncle to you. So many times when Rico or Tony wanted to run you out of town on a marble slab, I told them, 'Hands off Noir, he's family.' I had your back. More than once. Otherwise you would've been floating down the Mississippi in a barge full of soybeans and processed into tofu and eaten by skinny women and pooped out and floated out to sea. Is that what you want for yourself? To be sludge on the ocean floor?"

I suggested that I take him into the deal as a consultant. He snorted. "I had a cat once who was neutered, but he still went out at night and served as a consultant. Not me. Stop wasting my time."

I suggested that we go to Danny's and talk about it over a bowl of chicken noodle soup and a hot Reuben.

He thumped the pistol butt on the desk and wheezed from the effort. He whispered, "You got ten seconds to talk, Noir. You're trying to cut me out of a meal ticket, and I'm not gonna take that laying down."

I saw my opening.

I pointed out to him that *laying* is a transitive verb, it takes an object — you lay down your head on a pillow, but you yourself lie

15

down on a bed — so what he should've said was *lying down* — and Joey did not care to be corrected like he was back in the sixth grade at Immaculate Conception. He shifted in his seat as if to get better aim at my aorta, and he landed smack on those painful hemorrhoids and whimpered, and I grabbed his right wrist and twisted it and made him lay down his pistol on the table. And then I pinched his oxygen tube to make him lie down. Which he did. He laid his big noggin down on the desk, and his body relaxed, and he let a long hissy fart that smelled of fried automobile tires.

"Sweet dreams, pal." I crimped the tube for forty-five seconds, long enough to shift his synapses into neutral, and then released.

He opened his eyes and blinked. "What you doing with my gun?" he croaked.

"Just borrowing it for a day or two," I said.

"Oh," he said. "Okay."

I helped him to his feet. "Lulu LaFollette called, Joey. She's upset that you forgot you said you'd meet her at the Hotel Cranston. Room seven-sixteen. She's got her green chiffon nightie on, and she's all hot and sweaty thinking about doing the horizontal dance with you." He grinned and heaved himself to his feet. "My memory isn't what it used to be," he whispered. "Thanks,

16

Guy." And he lumbered off to perform amatory wonders on the buxom bombshell — who, for all I knew, was back home on her llama ranch in Stanley, North Dakota.

And a minute later, he was back. "Lulu who?"

"LaFollette."

"The name is familiar."

"The singer, Joey."

"Oh yeah."

And I put a hand on his shoulder and sang —

*Even those who write prose do it.*
*People wearing all their clothes do it.*
*Let's do it. Let's go to town.*
*Some intertwined centipedes do it.*
*In winter, even Swedes do it.*
*Let's do it. Let's go to town.*
*Gorillas deep in the mists do it,*
*Hanging by their palms.*
*True feminists do it,*
*Though they have qualms.*
*The lower halves of giraffes do it,*
*Even managers of office staffs do it,*
*Let's do it. Let's go to town.*

And he headed for the Cranston, a smiling man with a song in his heart, not the homicidal psychopath he was fifteen minutes previous. Love will do that to a man. And senile dementia. It has made Mr. Roast Beef a much nicer human being. It should happen to more people than it does.

Ten minutes later, more thumping on the door. It was Joey, all hot and bothered. "You sent me somewhere and I forgot where," he said. "How about you write it down on a slip of paper."

So his urge to canoodle with Lulu LaFollette was no longer strong enough to stick in his cerebellum. I said, "I was sending you home, Joey. Adele wants you to check on Pookie and Mr. Big Boy."

"What's wrong?" His eyes filled with tears. "Are they all right?"

Joey is quite devoted to his elderly Siamese. He called me once, devastated, when Pookie disappeared, and I joined him, walking up and down West 7th Street calling "Pookie Pookie Pookie." A reputable PI and a 340-pound man in a black pinstriped suit walking to and fro and calling out "Pookie Pookie Pookie." From such little deeds of kindness had I built the loyalty that made Joey hesitate to blow me a new buttonhole.

I told him the cats were fine. "They have a little fever, and Adele wants you to come home and slip a thermometer up their butts."

He wrung his hands and whimpered something about not knowing what he would do if his babies got sick and died, and out the door he went. It was a whole other Joey from the guy aiming the pistol at my sternum. I made a mental note: *Joey — vulnerable to extreme anxiety about cats. In case of emergency, ask him if Pookie is feeling better.*

# 2
## Naomi, O My Naomi

I stored Joey's pistol in the top drawer of my file cabinet, behind a bottle of booze and under a copy of *Playboy* ("Ten-page Pictorial: Women of the American Dairy Association") — and I locked up the office and took the elevator down to the lobby. The organic fair-trade vegetarian restaurant Bright Morning Stars had a CLOSED sign in the window, having gone out of business two weeks before. Inside, the handcrafted chairs were stacked on the sustainable tables, the traditional quilts hanging on the walls were gone, ditto the sensitive wait-staff. St. Paul is a meatloaf-and-mashed-spuds kind of town, not big on lentils or groats and we prefer experienced olive oil. The Yarnery had closed, and the artisan sausage shop, The Wienery, replaced by Boyd's Pet Rental ("Dogs, cats, birds, fish — low monthly rates — nice selection of colors"). I walked into the dim and cavernous Brew Ha Ha coffee shop just as Sharon the barista cranked up her espresso machine with a whisper of steam that sounded suggestive to me, like the sighs of a woman I knew long ago who liked me to rub palm oil on her back. I think her name was Patty. I leaned up against the counter and ordered an ordinary coffee. Small. Black.

"How about a pumpkin latte?" she says. "Live it up for once."

"Why put pie in your coffee? You're supposed to drink your coffee while eating your pie, not dump the pumpkin in it. Just give me a black coffee. No flavoring. Except coffee beans."

"Not even nutmeg?"

I shook my head.

"You want sprinkles with that?"

"No, thanks. No whipped cream either. Coffee."

"Okay, Pops."

The place was crawling with art students from St. Paul Art School, Market Street (SPASMS), also known as Simply Pray And Send Money Soon, housed in the old Great Northern warehouse on Market Street. All you need to know about SPASMS, you could see in the students' work hanging on the Ha Ha walls, dark blotchy images of

21

blighted buildings, junkyards, deserted highways, and drunks on buses, rich with teen angst, the revenge of the incompetent on the lighthearted. Twenty or thirty students sat typing at laptops, texting on cell phones, talking their odd jittery talk — *So she was like, Huh? And he goes like, Whatever. And I'm like, No way. And she's like, Way.* Kids with baggy low-slung pants and backward baseball caps and active vocabularies of about five hundred words. A generation of the Ten-second Glance, the Snack, the Quick Read, the Sound Bite, the Tweet. Everything snappy and quippy. No tolerance for the ponderous and pretentious. I like that. Lots in code. *OMG. LOL. LMAO. WTF.* You're either *awesome* or *gross.* Either *cool* or *total loser.* I don't claim to be awesome, but for the right woman I would make an effort in that direction. Especially a girl who is laughing her ass off.

Like the Chicago girl I met ages ago in New York when I worked in Harry's Shoes and I showed her some fancy knee-high leather boots. She couldn't choose between two pairs and asked me if she should pick the sexy ones or the comfortable ones. I was twenty-one. I said, "You're already sexy. Pick the ones that make you feel good." Next thing I knew, we were in the changing room, and I was kissing her pale trembling thighs, and she burst out laughing. She had silky blond hair, and she sat, legs apart, shrieking and writhing, the erotic and the comic all one thing to her. My supervisor, Hugh, threw open the door and asked what was I doing — "Customer service," I said, and the girl laughed harder. Ah, youth, heedless youth — no woman my age has time for an amorous shoe salesman anymore.

A youth with a tinge of beard walked by doing fist bumps (*Hey, wassup?*) and plopped down next to a girl who pointed at her computer screen and a video of a cat walking into a glass door, falling down, getting up, walking solemnly away, as if this were a yoga position. "Cool," he said. They all had glittery metal hanging from their eyebrows, eyelids, lips, earrings all around their ears, metal plugs in their noses and tongues — it looked like they had fallen face-first into the tackle box. *Taptaptaptaptap.* The sheer volume of data transmission was staggering, Facebook updates, posting, texting, e-mailing, and there at the counter, waiting for his latte, a kid gabbing on the phone about his girlfriend, Terry, who'd dumped him at a party so he drank ten beers and a wallop of vodka and smoked two big fat reefers and came home and puked and now he was feeling better except for the headache, and then he said, "Gotta run, Mom. Later. Love you, too." And didn't run. He stood there and typed on his iPhone a Facebook update about how he was thinking about getting started on his screenplay about a small town invaded by pockmarked one-eyed zombie clones carrying a mutant virus that turns human flesh into toxic fungus.

Poor kids. They'd talked their parents into fronting the dough for art school so the kiddos could prolong adolescence a few more years. That's what MFA means. My Fascinating Adolescence. It's the Montessori generation, so everybody wins a blue ribbon, everyone's ideas are valid, everyone is on a journey, we're all talented, all roads lead to Art. The girls dress like streetwalkers and the boys like drug dealers, and they adopt the slang of the black underworld, which they have no firsthand knowledge of, and they're okay with that. They're okay with not knowing much of anything. I envy them that. They had Ritalin and Prozac to smooth out the rough spots, and now they sit drinking expensive warmed milk and building elaborate shrines to themselves on

Facebook as they try to live creative lives and be free and do good in the world, which is why we need Mexicans to sneak across the border and mow our lawns and clean our toilets — so the kids can sit around looking in a mirror and feeling like artists, though none of them can so much as draw a pink petunia in a plaster pot. But so what? The world belongs to the young and the daring, the avid, the adventurous, and when I hear young women laugh, as I always do in the Ha Ha, I think of the Chicago girl and her pale ticklish thighs. I wonder where she is now. (In her mid-sixties, that's where.)

"You're looking good this morning," said Sharon. "Very dapper. I like those green socks." I smiled and dropped two bucks into her tip jar.

"I'm from the era when people used to get dolled up, babes. Ever since Liberace died, dressing up has gone out of style."

"Who was Liberace?" she asked.

"He was a pianist with big flashy teeth and diamond rings who came out on stage in a brown sealskin coat and a matching Rolls-Royce," I said. "And then a white sealskin coat and a white Rolls-Royce. And then black. He wasn't afraid to be the show-off. He played piano with cascading arpeggios under a blazing candelabra and he grinned constantly, showing off his dental work — he was Mr. Showmanship and gay as the day he was born and nobody cared because behind that grin were even more grins. He was a nut and people loved him for it."

"Before my time," she said. "Oh, by the way, a fatso in a seersucker suit came in looking for you. He looked really steamed. I meant to call you, but then I got busy."

"No problem. A little misunderstanding. Guy by the name of Joey. He's gone."

"He a friend of yours?"

"Not a friend as Webster's would define *friend,* but you wouldn't want him for an enemy."

"I heard that he once tried to suffocate somebody with a plastic dry-cleaning bag."

"True. I was there. I was the one who kept him from killing the guy. A real jackass by the name of Larry B. Larry. He got his start sucking dimes out of pay toilets — that's how no good he was. A real sleazebag. He was no lawyer, but he had business cards printed up that looked lawyerly and said LARRY B. LARRY, COUNSELOR AT LAW & PERSONAL REPRESENTATIVE. Went around in a spiffy pinstriped suit and bowtie and two-tone shoes, and he had a voice like corn oil. His specialty was trolling for people

26

who'd found flies in their ointment. Mr. Larry would contact the ointment company and threaten a lawsuit. He worked on commission, 50 percent. Once he found an old lady who'd swallowed a fly at a lutefisk dinner and thought she'd die, so he went to the offices of Amalgamated Lutefisk and told them the lady had suffered traumatic brain damage and was about to file suit for $350,000. Well, Amalgamated thought it over and decided that rather than going to trial in front of a jury that might include people who'd had bad lutefisk experiences and run the risk of a large judgment, why not negotiate with the guy, so they offered him $75,000, and he snapped it up like a fox grabs a chicken. He was a real stinker. On that particular occasion when he almost got plasticated, he was telling me a dirty joke about a Catholic priest and an altar boy, and Joey overheard it, a slur on his faith, and stuffed the plastic bag down Mr. Larry's throat and wrapped a coat hanger around his neck and commenced to throttle him. His eyes were spinning, his lunch was coming out his nostrils. I pried Joey's fingers from the jerk's neck and extracted the bag from his gullet. I said, 'Joey, why waste a homicide rap on a crum bum like Larry? Why spend your twilight years in a six-by-ten cell just for the pleasure of wiping this yo-yo from the earth?' And Joey let him go. And he was grateful to me. 'Yer right,' he says. 'Pookie and Big Boy would die without me.' He did me a lot of favors after that. Joey knew all the cops. He passed on useful information to me for years, out of gratitude. One thing about hoodlums, they do remember who did them a good turn. Also who did them dirt. But now Joey's eighty-two, and he's down with a nasty case of dementia. It can hit a gangster just like it hits your mama, except she is not packing a pistol. So I had to take Joey's gun off him upstairs, and now I got to figure out how to give it back."

A terrific story, and when I finished, I looked around for Sharon, and she was fishing in a big glass jar for raspberry biscotti. This happens to me more and more these days. I'm telling a fascinating tale to an attractive young woman, and halfway through it I realize that she is checking her phone for text messages. *Have I become a garrulous old fart who people think* Oh no not him *when they see me approach?*

One of many questions on my mind that cold afternoon.

And also: *How had Joey gotten wind of my secret?*

*Had I talked in my sleep?*

*Had I slept with the wrong person? Had someone spotted my vacation brochure with a circle around the August 24 "Northern Nirvana" voyage of the* MS Bel Canto, *from Oslo for fourteen fun-filled nights in the fjords north to Tromsø and back, and my heavy underlining of "the King Haakon Penthouse Suite with king-size bed and 800 sq. ft. balcony with hot tub"?*

If an elderly halfwit like Joey had sniffed out my secret, then half of St. Paul might be onto me, too. Maybe Lieutenant Mc-Cafferty, who has often promised me a one-way ticket to Winnipeg, or Gene Williker of the *Dispatch,* who's made a career out of smacking down the upwardly mobile. Mc-Cafferty was still sore that I tripped him up in the St. Olaf Choir case. They had sung in Acapulco for a convention of Lutheran stockbrokers, and he nabbed them at the airport with a suitcase stuffed with mari-juana, street value of $1. 2 million. I proved that the airline had delivered the wrong bag. Also that the marijuana was alfalfa. Street value: a buck seventy-five. And McCaf-ferty's boss reassigned him to traffic control for thirty days, and he stood there in his neon orange vest waving his arms in the middle of Sixth and St. Peter and cursing me with every gin-flavored breath. Likewise Gene Williker would be thrilled to blow me out of the water, having fallen for the choral bust (WHERE THERE'S SMOKE, THERE'S CHOIR: OLAF KIDS CAUGHT WITH STASH OF HASH) and gotten a sixty-day demotion to the obit division. I could picture him and McCafferty sniffing down my trail and putting the thumbscrews to witnesses and writing the indictment and then the sixty-five-point headline in the Monday paper (NOIR NABBED IN DRUG SCAM, FORMER B-GIRL SINGS TO GRAND JURY). Here I was, after years of low cash flow, sitting on a beautiful secret with the potential to boost me out of the Ditch of Despond and set me up on Easy Street and buy me the luxury cruise, the Corvette, the cashmere coat, the condo in Cancún, the cosmetic surgery, that I had long coveted, and bring wholehearted love into my life instead of the grudging attention of lonely women with self-esteem issues. All thanks to Naomi Fallopian, my old pal from back when I was a part-time bouncer at the Kit Kat Klub.

Ah, Naomi. Woman of my dreams. Song of my heart. Light of my loins. My rescuer.

I took the elevator back up to twelve, half expecting to see Joey lurking by my door, his faculties regained, waiting to crush me.

I tiptoed down the hall and slipped into the office and turned on the electric heater. Which I had bought for $45 off a goombah relocating to Florida so he could get involved in the lucrative transplant organ racket. A sheet of ice on the window made it look as if the Acme were underwater. I took a hair dryer out of the file cabinet and blasted the ice on the glass so as to let in more light, but it was no go. I hate dimness, especially in winter. It gives me a feeling of incarceration. I thought, *Guy, you have got to get out of this town, and Naomi is your ride.*

Naomi Fallopian hailed from Homer, Minnesota, the youngest of eleven children of a hog farmer and his wife, and came to St. Paul at age seventeen to attend Bible school. It was her daddy's wish. He was a fervent Baptist who when he went to town liked to stand outside the tavern singing "The Ninety-and-Nine" and handing out gospel tracts entitled "Where Will You Spend Eternity?" and as a consequence his baby daughter grew up curious about the sins of the flesh. She learned to dance the jitterbug swing. She learned to smoke Luckies and drink sloe gin. She earned a reputation as a very good kisser. So he shipped her off to Summit Bible College, where she roomed with a professor of New Testament

31

named Lyman Humble and his wife, Persis, who prayed morning and night and at every meal and every snack and every cup of coffee. They said grace if they took two aspirin and a sip of water. Naomi was restive at the Humbles. She went off to class in the morning (after Professor Humble had led the three of them in a long twisting labyrinth of prayer and a long march through the Book of Deuteronomy), wearing the requisite shapeless brown dress, and took a detour to a drugstore on Selby Avenue and bought a pack of smokes. She took off the brown dress, under which she wore a red dress with a swooping neckline, and she made the rounds of the gin mills along the avenue, Costello's and Schmutterer's and Nina's and the Common Good Cocktail Lounge, and strolled through each one with a tin cup and sang "She Is More to Be Pitied Than Censured," draping an arm around the drunks and letting them breathe on her, and earned enough money to buy herself breakfast and lunch and a couple of non-Christian novels. She liked to roost in a luncheonette at Grand and Lexington, sit in a back booth and eat apple fritters, and pore over Fitzgerald and Raymond Chandler and Anita Loos ("Show business is the best possible therapy for remorse") and was spotted one day by a fellow student who ratted on her, and she was hauled off to Chapel, where the entire student body gathered to pray for her soul, after which she was asked to repent, which she declined to do.

"You preach about love, but none of you has enough warmth in you to melt snow," she cried. "I don't know how much of the Bible is true and how much is just a bad dream, but I do believe that if Jesus lived in St. Paul, he wouldn't be sitting around in this school of sanctimony congratulating himself on what a nice person he is. He'd be walking up and down Selby Avenue just like I do."

And she marched out of Chapel and never returned, and when I met her three years later, she was dancing seven nights a week at the Kit Kat Klub near the Union Depot, a murky after-hours joint that catered to barge hands and railroad men who needed to get hammered and look at bare skin and shove dollar bills in the dancers' underwear. The Folies Bergère it was not. Most of the dancers were long past prime and starting to sag, and Naomi was fresh-faced and perky and bouncy and she reminded those old galoots of girls they wished they had dated in high school and there she was doing the Hitchhiker in a sequinny G-string with smiley-face stickers on her nipples that she peeled off, and concluded her performance by tossing the G-string into the crowd. I took a fatherly interest in her and protected her from Dave the comedian ("Hey, who wants to see my tits????") and Jervis the manager, who liked to stroll into the dressing room without knocking, and the mouth breathers who hunkered up close to the footlights, gaping at her, stuffing ten-dollar bills into her butt crack. The crisp new bills scratched her there, and she sometimes asked me to apply Vaseline to the affected area, which I did, respectfully, in a brisk businesslike manner, taking no liberties. I always bought her a beer after her shift and advised her on career matters — she wanted to become an actress and get into the movies — and I persuaded her to enroll at the University of Minnesota, and helped with her tuition, and I fended off her ex-boyfriends who hung around in the alley, pining. I told them, "She's moving on, fellows, so wish her well and count yourselves lucky to have known her and now get the hell out of here." She graduated from the U *magna non troppo* and I attended the ceremony and took her to dinner at Vescio's and urged her to apply for the Mary Magdalene fellowship at St. Kate's, and she did, and eventually she sort of drifted away, as so many do when they get a Ph.D.

She quit stripping and joined the women's studies department at the university and wrote a book, *Post-Masculine Dimensions,* in which she held my gender responsible for all human suffering — MENtal illness, MENstrual cramps, disappointMENt, MENopause, HISterectomies, MALEvolence, ballistics, penal colonies, dictators, prickly heat, et cetera. I bought ten copies and subscribed to *Estrogen Times* and read the articles she wrote, and a few years later I got an e-mail: *Guy darling, it's your old friend from burlesque days (remember me?).* I did remember her, the way you'd remember the Washington Monument if you ever saw it lit up at night, or the French Quarter if you'd been lit up yourself. *I live over in Minneapolis now, near Dinkytown, and I have a problem. Could you help?*

I met her at Al's Breakfast Nook, and she was stunning as ever, though she wore black horn-rimmed glasses and a black pinstripe suit to mute her allure. She missed the old life, she said: the smell of cheap gin and cigars, the gutbucket music, the grunts and whoops, and the rank odor of men in rut. "I felt empowered by showing my body to men. I felt no shame whatsoever. The power a girl has when she dares to undress is breathtaking. All those sad old faces turned up toward me in dazed wonderment as if they'd never seen a bare breast before, let alone a matched pair, and those gnarly hands reaching up for the flying G-string, and that look of transfiguration when I showed them what they had hoped to see. I felt so *iconic.* I fed their dreams. I gave them a beautiful sense of self-worth that they could carry back to the switchyards and endure the cold wind off the river and the back-breaking work of loading boxcars and barges. I feel deracinated in academia. Uprooted. And the pay is miserable. How can a person live on thirty grand a year unless you're a nun? I want to ride first-class on the California Zephyr to San Francisco and stay at the Huntington and have oysters and champagne for breakfast and sleep on Egyptian sheets with a fabulous thread count and have someone bring me coffee in the morning and a massage in the afternoon!"

Sitting over breakfast with her, I realized that my feelings for her were no longer paternal. I had fallen in love, *boom,* like an anvil dropping from a tree.

*I could take care of the coffee,* I thought. *And the massage. And I could sleep next to you and keep you from falling out of bed.*

The problem she wished me to solve had to do with her boyfriend, a novelist (unpublished) named Scott Marigold who believed that someone was scheming to steal his work and so he wrote in code, and now he'd forgotten the code, and he was bereft and had lost all interest in life, and would I please find a cryptographer who could decipher the work? She showed me a line:

BIQ SUATRO MEECH KWERTY NISK REMPLON NAMLEREP TRIXLY SWISK THEBBRILIP PO ENNER SKWILM.

"Child's play," I said. "This passage here, *Biq suatro meech kwerty,* and so forth, means 'She had big bazooms, and I loved it when she spread peanut butter on them and knelt over me and whopped them upside my head.'"

"Really? That doesn't sound like Scott."

"It's what he wrote."

"How could you figure it out so fast?"

"I'm a savant. No social skills and I've never been able to win the love of a real woman, but I'm a whiz with complex puzzles."

She put her hand on mine and said, "Oh, Guy —"

I said, "Don't worry about me, darling,

I'm glad you're happy. Really."

"I didn't say I was happy." Big tears in her eyes. "I think Scott has found someone else. We have sex and I say 'Thank you' and he says 'No problem.' Doesn't that strike you as peculiar?"

I nodded. A man who's just had sex with Naomi should be breathless, stunned, astonished, singing "My Way" in French.

"I wish he'd say 'It was my pleasure' or 'I love you' or 'On a scale of one to ten, that was a nine-point-five' — anything but 'No problem.' 'No problem' is what the carry-out boy at the Super Valu says when you thank him for loading the groceries into your trunk. I am not a bag of groceries, am I?"

We said good-bye, and she clung to me for a long, wonderful moment. "I need you, Guy," she said. I thought, *Baby, what do you need with a third-rate detective thirty years older, with hair loss issues and flabby abs and droopy delts?* But if she needed me, then she needed me, and who was I to argue?

That very evening Naomi discovered a blue silk garter belt in Mr. Marigold's computer bag, which he claimed not to know where it came from, which was not believable, and she told him they were through, and he said,

38

"No problem," and she tried to strangle him with the belt and almost succeeded. The next morning it was on the front page:

**U WOMAN PROF TRIES TO THROTTLE LOVER; ARRAIGNED ON FELONY ASSAULT CHARGE; COLLEAGUES SAY: "SHE SURE WAS DIFFERENT."**

And the next morning Birch Bergquist of Bergquist, Batten, Bicker, Buttress & Bark, offices two floors below me in the Acme Building, called to say she was representing Naomi and could I come down a.s.a.p. for a confab?

I had bumped into Miss Bergquist occasionally in the elevator and assumed she was someone's receptionist — the pouty lips, the bluish eye shadow, the blouse slightly unbuttoned — but here she was, a full-fledged attorney, in her leatherbound-book-lined office, certificates on the wall, behind an oak desk the size of a billiard table, and wearing a Mount Rushmore tank top so tight you could keep close track of her respiration. Those four guys never looked so good, especially Washington and Lincoln. Just looking at her gave me chest pains. No signs of brassiere seams whatsoever. I could imagine her saying, "Help me off with this," as we stood one evening in the penthouse suite of the *Bel Canto,* candles flickering beside the bed.

"It's my day off," she said. "I was heading for my boyfriend's stepmother's ex-husband's birthday party when Naomi called from jail."

The mention of a boyfriend woke me right up, as if she had jerked my leash and said "Sit." Nonetheless she was a dreamboat. Good skin care, good posture, and an outstanding tank top.

"Naomi's the impulsive sort, and she and that jerk novelist had been on the outs for a long time. I'm talking to the DA's office to get this reduced to simple assault, but the DA is a lady, and she's had a spate of sexual harassment cases involving high-profile men, and she sees this as a chance to show she can prosecute a woman too, so we may have to go to trial on attempted homicide, which is ludicrous, but there you are. I need you to dig up the dirt on the boyfriend and find out where the garter belt came from."

No problemo. Mr. Marigold was no novelist, just a doink with novelist hair and a big attitude, and the garter belt came from a topless dancer named Ruby Doobie who worked the BoomBoom Room of the Xtasy Club, a seedy sex warehouse in Minneapolis, and who'd been dancing on the boy-friend's lap. Her real name was Kirsten Hammersmith. She told me that the garter belt was not silk but a breakaway type made of thin tissue. It wasn't strong enough to strangle a tree toad. I also discovered that Mr. Marigold visited pornographic websites for men who fantasize about big-bosomed women who smack you for not eating your vegetables. And he sent pictures of himself, naked, to numerous Congresswomen.

This all came out at the trial. Miss Bergquist portrayed Naomi as a good teacher, a caring colleague, an erudite scholar, a cat lady, a reader of scholarly journals, hardly a homicidal type, and the prosecution portrayed her as a slut who put herself through grad school by showing her tits. They played a video of her twirling her pink-tipped twosome and lip-synching to Henny Penny's "Back It Up, Baby, and Push" — but what stuck with the jury was the testimony of a woman named Herta Goethe who Mr. Marigold had paid $150 to rub anchovy paste all over his body. The jury was out for eighteen minutes. Innocent.

At the acquittal party Naomi gave me a big hug that went on and on, and there was real heat in her coral-blue eyes. "If not for you, I'd be in an orange jumpsuit, swabbing out toilets," she said. "I owe my life to your ace detective work, my darling Mr. Noir."

Not strictly true. The men of the jury appreciated the "Back It Up, Baby, and Push" video and also Naomi's translucent blouse, whose top three buttons she kept unbuttoning and rebuttoning, offering glimpses of two freckled free-range breasts that the jurymen maybe hoped would fall out, and maybe acquittal would make the defendant jump up and down and those puppies would leap over the fence. But I wasn't about to argue, not with her pressing herself against me in an interesting way, kissing me behind the ear, a spot that's always been sensitive to me. She whispered, "You're archetypal in a way I could get to like in a big hurry. If you kissed me forcefully right now, I might not resist as much as you'd expect an associate professor of women's studies to do."

Her voice was low and thrilling: "I don't know anybody who gets me the way you do. And after I met you again at Al's, Mr. Marigold lost whatever allure he ever had, that big nothing. I've thought of you hundreds of times since then. I've got a business proposition that might interest you. Let's get together," she said. "Tuesday. And please — call me Naomi."

And then she stood up and hoisted her dress up over her head and danced on a tabletop in a thong so small, the laundry instructions had to be abbreviated ("Hnd wsh cld wtr") — danced to "I Can't Get Enough of Your Sweet Kanaka" — and when the song ended, she hopped down off the table and into my arms and whispered, "Don't forget. Tuesday. Meet you at the Five Spot. In the back." I was stunned. Still am, thinking about it. You could've hit me with a baseball bat, and I would've said, "Thank you."

# 3

# A WINTER AFTERNOON IN THE FIVE SPOT SALOON

Tuesday was one of those grim February days when winter seems permanent in Minnesota and everyone you see is bundled up so you can't tell men from women, not that it matters when it's so cold, you wouldn't know what to do about gender anyway. Your lungs ache, your face is numb, your heart is a lump of anthracite in your chest. The sky is an aluminum lid on the frozen land; it says: *Surrender hope all ye poor huddled masses and wretched refuse who hunker here.* Steam pours from the implacable stone buildings of downtown St. Paul as if the end of the world were nigh. The Five Spot is three blocks from the Acme, and I ankled down the icy walk in a primate crouch, maintaining a low center of gravity, trying to keep myself balanced, like an acrobat poised on a teacup atop a rubber ball strapped to a roller skate, knowing that one slip could usher me into a world of lower back pain and Oxycontin and a physical therapist named Karen saying, "Good job!" if I'm able to put one foot in front of the other. So I kept my eyes glued to the treacherous sidewalk and then realized I had walked three blocks *past* the Five Spot, so I took care of some business on Exchange Street — stopped at the Beethoven Apartments to buzz 4R to ascertain that Mr. Louie Louey was there, as required by his bondsman Barry (The Handshake) O'Halloran, who'd put up the ten grand to spring Louie from Ramsey County jail where he was down for killing spotted owls for owlburgers. He was in 4R, napping. The Beethoven, by the by, was where Sugar O'Toole lived before she dumped me for Wally and moved to his trout farm near Willmar and also where Beatrice Olsen liaised with her secret lover and then dumped me for him, the librettist Brett Brackett, in case you are interested. A building I have many times looked at and wept.

From the Beethoven I passed under the dim flickering marquee of the Fitzgerald Theater (LOS PAMPAS CASA COMPANEROS, 5 PM ATURDAY), where I once attended martial arts movies with a lady shot-putter from St. Peter named Roxanne (Rocky) Nimitz. "You try any funny stuff with me and I'll launch you into space," she said. She was a big-boned gal, 285 pounds, close-cropped hair, disciple of Ayn Rand, All-American in women's track, and proud of her ability to fart "My Country, 'Tis of Thee" in perfect pitch, time after time. She was saving her affection for the right man, and I was grateful not to be him. The Fitzgerald had also been the home of *A Prairie Home Companion,* but people lost interest in corn fiddles and Ole and Lena jokes and paeans to Main Street U.S.A., and the show became *Los Pampas Casa Companeros,* which means *"The Friend of the House on a Flat Place,"* and it switched over to salsa music and mariachi bands and olive-skinned women in thigh-high boots with stiletto heels, and a host named Garcia Columbo told stories of village life in Yucatan and the show got popular again. It gained cachet among the young and restless and became a radio show you'd like to be heard listening to.

I inched along the killer sidewalks between high mounds of glazed snow past Eisenberg's Fruits, past the police station and Central Presbyterian, where I once attended a Sunday service with Beatrice when we were trying to not break up and the sermon was basically "Live and let live, we are all human," which, if that's what Presbyterians really believe, I'd sign up for Adult Bible Study. Here in Minnesota, people are anything but tolerant. They are vicious sociopaths on the freeways and will speed up to prevent you from merging into their lane ahead of them. And if you happen to catch one in a sinful act, they hate you for it. I once saw a Republican legislator shoplifting ballpoint pens in Walgreens, and he caught me watching him and he introduced a so-called Privacy Act, which requires a sleuth to inform a person if he or she is being surveilled. They attached this as an amendment to a bill providing warm lunches for wounded veterans, and it passed on a voice vote, and suddenly I am on the dark side of the law, and Lieutenant McCafferty has one more sharp stick to poke in my eye. Likewise, the young Lutheran pastors hanging around Miller's soda fountain on Como Avenue near the seminary. I was tailing a seminarian named Gibbs who Barnes & Noble believed was shoplifting the texts of other religions and dumping them in recycling, and I sat near this gang of clerics and listened to them savage their senior pastors mercilessly, ridiculing their wimpy sermons, imitating their pious drony voices — and then they spotted me taking notes and came after me like hounds on a possum and there was a Laying On of Hands and a Snatching of the Notebook, and when I went to start my car, it wouldn't. Someone had poured water in the gas tank. Minnesotans imagine they are nicer than other Americans, and if you point out that they are not, they'll put sand in your meatballs.

ANYWAY.

I arrived half-frozen at the Five Spot, and no Naomi, so I perched at the bar. The Five Spot is dim and lustrous, like a Rembrandt painting, especially if you've had a whiskey or two — the dark wood, the brass trim, the glow of the lights, the old Rembrandt faces. I had a dollar fifty in my pocket, I'd have to count on Naomi to buy the drinks. Hard times in private eyedom. I'd had one case all month — *one case* — lady asked me to nail her cheating no-good husband, and I made the rounds of the gin mills and bordellos, and she calls me five hours later to say that he'd run off with someone he met on Facebook and good riddance. "Anyway," I said, "You owe me a hundred fifty dollars for my troubles." She laughed a hearty bronchial laugh, and then my ear was filled with dial tone. Rule number one in the Famous Shamus Handbook: *Get the money up front.* A basic rule, along with *Never be rude to a waitress from whom you have just ordered soup.* — Anyhow, I was flat broke. "What's wrong? Somebody shoot your dog?" says Jimmy the bartender, swabbing the bar, his sandy hair brushed back, starched white apron, bowtie in place, a neutral look on his pale mug. "Gimme a glass of water," says me. On the jukebox, the Surf Men singing "Laura":

*L-a-u-r-a*
*Beautiful city on the Pacific coast*
*And you are the lady I love the most*
*On this warm and sunny day.*
*Minnesota is so far away.*
*Guess I'll stay.*

The Five Spot is classic art deco, mirrors everywhere so you can stare at people without looking directly at them. There were three others in the joint, an old man studying his reflection in the bottom of his glass, and a florist named Ray on an extended lunch break, and a woman in a navy blue suit, weeping into her gin rickey. "Her kid didn't get into a top-ranked kindergarten," Jimmy whispered. And suddenly there was Naomi, like a genie in mink, leaning down, saying "Hi, darling," her remarkable cleavage eight inches away, like two Bosc pears in a Modigliani still life.

She ordered a white wine, dry, and led me back to a booth by the door to the storeroom. As she walked, her golden wool gown undulated on her womanly hips like curtains in a light breeze. I wanted to open the curtains and let the sun shine.

She hung up her mink and slid into the booth and patted the bench beside her, and I sat down and she leaned in so close, I could feel the breeze from her eyelashes' flutter. She said, "Here's the deal, babes. Between you and me, I'm on to a simple brilliant business scheme that can earn millions of dollars in a big hurry. The sort of idea that people daydream about, but in this case it's for real. I have quit my job in women's studies, and I got all the pieces in place, and it's ready to go, the motor is running, and I need you to work security. If you want in, I'll tell you the whole story. But I want you to know up front — I had to swipe the idea from a jerk who swiped it from somebody else, which I did because why should a jerk have all the luck, and now he's sicced a goon named Larry B. Larry on me, and I need you to run interference. And it's dangerous, Guy. Because there's big money involved. So I want you to know that. This guy will stop at nothing."

"Larry B. Larry, the shyster lawyer who isn't a lawyer. I know him well. Know him like a mongoose knows a cobra."

"He's left two ugly messages in voice mail, about putting my tits in a wringer."

"He's a rough customer, babes. He put himself through a mail-order law school by stealing money from geezers who'd forgotten their own names but remembered their PIN numbers. He managed a local thrash band called Cold Reptiles, which became Croutons of Abuse. A band that stomped on their fans' fingers and sang about cruelty to animals but in real life were vegans. Mr. Larry is a creepy, bone-headed guy with pinkish eyes and a bad overbite and wears a ring with a rhinestone the size of a cashew. Splashes himself with lawyer cologne and leases a two-room office suite in the Shagmire Tower with framed photos of local celebs and a shag carpet made of old toupees. Tried to hire me once to follow his exwife around and knock down the guy she was keeping company with. I told him, 'I don't hit people for a living. I only hit people for personal spite. Not for money, thank you. My elevator doesn't stop at that floor.' So what did he do, the jerk? He glanced over my right shoulder and smiled as if someone were approaching, and when I glanced back, he bopped me on the chin. And then he laughed. I went to poke him in the snoot, and he whipped out a hatchet and cut a rope — I hadn't noticed it there behind me — which released a powerful hydraulic spring that sprang up, yanking a noose that I had inadvertently stepped in, and suddenly I was hanging by my left ankle. The old Sprung Leg Trap trick: I'd fallen for it. It was humiliating. Like stepping into an open manhole. The brute laughed onion breath in my face and inquired if I cared to reconsider the offer. There was a smirk on his big mug that didn't belong there. I lashed out with my right foot and plonked him in the gonads, and he grunted *Hunnhhh* like a dying water buffalo and collapsed and lay there agitating for a few minutes, long enough for me to cut the rope and escape.

"He never forgot that kick. For the past fifteen years since I rang his chimes, I've been the victim of late-night pizza deliveries and calls from telemarketers and political fund-raisers, which is Larry B. Larry paying me back for getting his nuts jingled. And, perhaps thanks to me, the man is childless. There is no Larry B. Larry, Junior. Anyway, yes, I do know the man."

"Good," she said. "I don't want to know him any better than I already do." And she put her hand on my knee. "Let me tell you how you and I are going to find the Good Life, babes. French designer clothes and a deluxe apartment in a doorman building and travel all over the world in unparalleled comfort." She smiled. I did notice that she referred to "we" and she did mention "a deluxe apartment" and not two deluxe apartments. One apartment. My skin tingled at the thought. Actually, many thoughts, a procession of them, racing by, many of them involving nakedness and heavy breathing and her saying, "When two people are very much in love —" etc. It sounded to me like a proposal of marriage. "I am all yours," I said, and I meant it.

# 4
## A BEAUTIFUL BEAUTIFUL IDEA

"It's the most effective weight-loss product ever known to man, and it's one hundred percent natural. You may doubt me, but it's true. Poor people have known about it for centuries, and now we'll make it available to the rich." She leaned in close to my ear. "Tapeworms," she said. "A special breed of tapeworms. You swallow a large reddish capsule, the worms hatch in your stomach, you eat all you like, they devour eighty-five percent of it, and you shrink to skin and bones, you take a little yellow pill, and you poop the worms out. It's simple, it's perfect, it does the job, and I've got a worm supplier, a man named Ishimoto. He's promised to produce a half-million red capsules in the next eighteen months.

"Americans spend sixty billion dollars a year on weight-loss stuff. Most of it a waste of money. I mean, the secret of weight loss is simple: eat less and move around more.

Everybody with a brain knows what to do: cut out bread, cut out butter and cheese, skip dessert, take long, brisk walks. But instead people lavish money on 'diet' foods and 'programs' and creams and gels and vitamins and get caught in a spiral of guilt and shame. Those actresses at the Oscars: each one skinnier than the next. In Los Angeles, a size one is considered medium. And the movies set the standard for glamour. To be beautiful today, you've gotta have two sticks for legs, a sunken belly, tits like ginger snaps, and a long swanlike neck with only your spine and gullet in it, otherwise you are Old & Fat & Washed Up."

She continued.

"The American obsession with youth and skinniness. It's tragic. Rich people buy powerful pills to jack up their metabolism to that of adolescent hummingbirds, but the pills have terrible side effects: they cause Nocturnal Excess Eating Disorder, and you wake up at four a.m. with empty ice cream cartons in your bed, so you have to go to a NEED support group and sit in a circle of folding chairs with weepy people in a church basement and share your sad stories about feelings of inadequacy going back to when you walked naked into the showers after ninth-grade gym and someone grabbed your belly roll and called you Porky and the nickname stuck to you for three painful years until you enlisted in the Marines and got the nickname Psycho.

"Rich people fly off to chop shops in Manhattan or L.A. to have their jiggly parts excised by smooth-talking surgeons and come out looking like Mongol mummies with a permanent look of alarm on their faces, and they have to wear a turtleneck and a serape to hide the hideous scars. Maybe the butt reduction comes out uneven, so they have to wear orthopedic pants with support pads in the cheeks to help them sit up straight. And their navel is now up in their armpit, so they can't wear sleeveless dresses.

"Rich people go on weird diets: lichen on RyKrisp and a soup made from birch bark — and they lose a few pounds and then black out. And in the morning, their bed is full of empty ice cream cartons. It's a wicked circle."

Naomi reached down into her bosom.

"And now here's this: Elongate."

She held out a clear plastic envelope containing a reddish gelatin capsule.

"Take this, and in two weeks you will begin to see the difference. *Eat what you like — gorge yourself on creamy desserts, cheesy omelets, half-pound hamburgers, giant car-tons of onion rings.* You will continue to lose weight until you take this." She held out a small yellow pill. "This cleans you out. Completely. Stay close to a toilet for a few hours, and when stuff comes out of you, don't look at it, just flush."

I opened the envelope and held the red capsule in the palm of my hand. I felt like Wilbur Wright watching Orville soar in the biplane at Kitty Hawk. Like John Logie Baird looking at the flickering image on his 1927 television. Or Frank Colton looking at Enovid, the first oral contraceptive, in 1952, and thinking about all the women who would sleep with him if they could only get their hands on this.

"You're looking at the cure for American obesity," she said. "A life saver."

"You've taken these?"

She grinned. "I used to have three chins and weigh 180 pounds, baby. My nickname in Bible school was Bubbles. I worked in a pizza joint. Pizzas the size of truck tires, and I ate the leftovers. And then I met a gynecologist named Buddy. He's the one who got me into stripping. He loved me, or parts of me, but not the fat parts, so he of-fered me these pills, not knowing what was in them, only that they had worked for him.

He'd gotten up to 380 and needed a motor-
ized cart to get around, and when I met
him, he was 168 and a men's senior hand-
ball champ. I took the pills and lost 70
pounds and gained a new personality. I
became a third-wave feminist who wants to
posit a poststructuralist positivist model of
gender that embraces ambiguity and rejects
the binary handcuffs of the first-wave para-
digm. And I also want to be fabulously rich
and utterly gorgeous so that men are helpless in my presence. The worms made me
gorgeous, and they're going to make me
rich. And you, too, if you want in."

The way she said "in" — it sounded like
more than a business proposition. It suggested something physical, a merger, if you
will, or interpolation. My loins warmed at
the thought, my aging loins, and I felt a
quick, irrational stab of premature jealousy
— that if I showed insufficient enthusiasm,
she might locate a younger, more agile
private eye and engage him.

"I want in. It's all I want. To be in.
Completely in."

She blinked. "Here's how it works. The
pills are produced by Mr. Ishimoto in his
bio-lab in Robbinsdale. He was in the germ
warfare business and wanted to get into
something socially constructive. A set of

pills costs about forty cents to produce, the packaging is about fifteen dollars, and the marketing and overhead two hundred. They retail for fifteen hundred, and you do the math. It's mostly pure profit. Of which, you, my friend, will be in for two percent. If that's okay."

When you've been residing in a third-floor studio walkup at the Shropshire Arms and the water is rusty and the drain is slow and your upstairs neighbors copulate vigorously at two a.m. on a bed with squeaky wheels, why quibble over percentage points? Two percent of several million was fine by me.

We shook hands on the deal, and she set a canvas tote bag on the table and pulled out a canister with a Baggie inside, and some rather fat worms, slowly writhing around each other. "These are the queens," she said. "Extra specimens of our prime breeding stock. Your job is to guard it. Any safe place with a temp between forty-five and eighty-five Fahrenheit is fine. A cupboard, a box under your bed. There's an electric warmer in here for when you carry it outdoors. This is what Mr. Larry B. Larry is after."

In the bottom of the Baggie were what appeared to be grains of brown rice. "Eggs," she said. "Mr. Ishimoto will drop by once a week and collect them. You'll have to arrange a safe meeting place. Here." She handed me a tiny cell phone. "This is a dedicated number that connects you to his line and only to his line. If you should be captured, you can press zero, and the thing shoots pepper spray out the skinny end. Aim at their eyes, and they'll be in agony for an hour or so, long enough for you to tie them to a railroad track or whatever seems best at the time. Don't laugh. You may need it." And then she gave me a large red capsule.

I handed it back to her, and she took my hand and closed it over the pill and told me to swallow it.

"Now?"

"Think of it as caviar," she said. "Except it doesn't taste fishy at all, or wormy. And it's not that I don't adore you just as you are, darling Guy, but I want you to understand what we're dealing with. And I think that secretly you want to be skinny. Take these and in a few weeks you'll be shopping for clothes in the boys' department."

When it comes to eating tapeworm eggs, a man doesn't want to think too hard about it. It isn't an intellectual problem. I thought about Naomi and me sitting naked, flank to flank, in a hot tub, and my flanks not flabby but sleek and trim, my gut nice and flat, not needing to be sucked in, my jowls gone, and I closed my eyes, and down the hatch it went, a little bump on the epiglottis, and I chased it with her white wine — "Whoops, is it okay to drink?" She laughed and said the worms love alcohol.

I took a deep breath. I imagined snakes writhing in my innards. I tried to focus on Naomi and her general fabulousness, her minty breath, her playful fingers, the marvelous illicitries that we could enjoy, ignoring the bubbly sensation in my belly. Like gas bubbles but more urgent. I have always tried to avoid farting around women, knowing how they disapprove of such things. I crossed my legs and clenched my bowels and tried to think pure thoughts, but an unmistakable gas bubble was forming within. I excused myself and walked quickly, slightly bent, cheeks flexed, to the men's can and closed the door, and *whammo,* out it came, one of those sickly putrid farts that can clear a room in seconds.

Memory is tied to smell, and that fart, like Proust's slice of cake, reminded me of Beatrice Olsen and why she left me for Brett Brackett. (Pardon me while I digress.) We were in New York, and I had fallen for her like a soufflé in an earthquake, and she had written a hit musical, *Song of Ourselves,* about the *ménage à trois* of Ralph Waldo Emerson, Henry Thoreau, and Emily Dickinson hanging out with God, who is a good guy but not 100 percent certain of his own divinity. He feels godlike some days, and other days it's hit and miss. It was SRO in Seattle and Boston with their large Unitarian populations. And Beatrice got it in her head that *The Great Gatsby (The Musical)* would be her next work — she said, "High school kids love *Gatsby.* It has New York, alcohol, big parties, nice clothes, hopeless yearning, violence, everything meaningful to teenagers. It'll *kill* at the box office" — and she decided to move to St. Paul, it being Fitzgerald's hometown. She and I were closer than a couple of mice in a shot glass, but I hated to leave New York. (Maybe she hoped that moving to St. Paul would be a way to lose me, but I didn't pick up the cue.) I told her, "Darling — St. Paul is the city he was running away from. New York is where he was running *to* — *Gatsby* is no more about St. Paul than *Grapes of Wrath* is about Chardonnay. All you'll get in St. Paul is some unhappy flashbacks." But she was packed and ready to go, and so I bade farewell to the Upper West Side and caught the dog to St. Paul and hung out my shingle at the Acme Building.

(PRIVATE EYE. Surveillance. Background Checks. Marital Research. Reasonable rates. NO JOB TOO SMALL.)

She and I roosted in the honeymoon suite at the Commodore Hotel for three fun-filled weeks, and on our walks around Crocus Hill, she pointed out houses she fancied, which I thought meant we'd get hitched, and then one night after a few mai tais in the mirror-lined bar, we had a big argument. She was Unitarian and agnostic and believed that man is merely a teeming mass of electrons with no free will, no soul, no afterlife. Woman, on the other hand, has a soul and perhaps an afterlife, so long as the man dies first. That's what she told me. Okay, so two lovers have theological differences — not a problem, right? But just then I let the worst fart of my life, it smelled like a dead badger on an asphalt bonfire, and she cried, "Oh my God, go away" and I did — for several days — slept on my office couch and bathed at the Y — and though we tried to repair the breach, it didn't work. The smell of that fart stayed on her mind. She never sat close to me again. A week later she told me she needed "more space," and I knew what she was referring to. And two weeks later, when I called her to say I'd taken her toothbrush by mistake, it was her librettist, Brett Brackett, who answered the phone in the honeymoon suite, the dimwit who wrote "Daisy Buchanan / Was crazy. A man in / His right mind would've said, 'Rats!' / But not Jay Gatz. Oh Jay Gatz / In his pastel shirts and brown felt hats, / Black shoes, white spats. / His gala parties, his confident talk / And the green light shone at the end of the dock." Ira Gershwin he was not, just another yahoo with an urge to scribble. They finished the first act of *Gatsby* and sang it for potential backers and stank out the room, so they abandoned *Gatsby* and wrote *Dance with Your Daddy* instead, a musical marshmallow about fathers and daughters that the American public was starved for, and their ship came in, and I sat in my dingy office and prayed for a submarine. She became Beatrice Brackett, and they bought a big stone Cass Gilbert house on Summit Avenue, and there went my last shot at the Happily Married Life, dang it. She was a goddess of a woman with great alabaster hips and a magnificent rump who slept in the nude and so did I, and we spooned together like pigs in warm mud, sighing, nudging, feasting on proximity.

That's matrimony. You don't have to astound each other with brilliant quips or fabulous salad dressings or prowess with the Sunday *Times* crossword, you thrive on nearness. And I did. Our bodies fit perfectly together, belly to rump. And then that horrible fart, which drove us apart. I admit it smelled bad, like sewer gas, but when it was gone, she somehow couldn't forget it. I apologized over and over. I took antiflatulence pills. Gave up coffee, beans, tapioca, rutabagas, fried onions, all the known fart agents. I went to a twelve-step group for recovering farts (*Admit that your gasses are out of control. Take inventory of your expulsions. Make amends to those whom you have offended.*) but she was gone, gone, gone, married to a nickel-plated dope, Mr. Wrong, and I, who was destined to be her husband, fell into a life of aimless romances. Every so often I'd see them go wheeling by on their Italian racing bikes, or running in their French running duds, and I'd catch a whiff of methane. Science tells us that everyone creates several pints of intestinal gas per day and releases it in a dozen or so farts. The Queen of England farts, and so does Angelina Jolie. One reason people run is to release the gas outdoors. And then they can sit and discuss intellectual matters without suddenly smelling like a dead badger.

Naomi smiled up at me when I returned to the table from my long Proustian moment in the men's can. "I forgot to tell you about the side effects," she said. "Heightened libido and also gassiness. A cruel combination. But that's the price you pay for getting skinny." She gave me the tote bag and a brown envelope and said, "Don't spend it all in one place," and kissed me lightly on the ear and then the other ear. "I'm going to be gone for a while, writing a book. Oh Guy, I miss you so much already. This is the beginning of a beautiful friendship," she said. She took the enormous mink coat off a coat hook and disappeared into the arctic night. It bothered me the way she said "friendship." It sounded so matter-of-fact, as if we'd be playing canasta in a tearoom over scones. I was frankly hoping for much more.

"Quite a dame. What were those pills she gave you?" Jimmy said. "Looked like peyote. I took some of that stuff back in the eighties, and I was wandering around for three days lost in a fog thinking there were secret messages in the songs of the Grateful Dead. I listened to 'Attics of My Life' about eighteen thousand times. I thought *cloudy dreams unreal* contained the secrets of the universe. Never eat a cactus, that's my advice. If you want to get crazy, I recommend bourbon."

I stepped back into the men's room, farted again, and opened the envelope. I didn't count the money, but it was somewhere around $25,000 in hundreds. Nobody had ever laid a bundle like that on me before, ever. I held it in my two hands like a newborn baby. I owed two grand in back rent to my landlady, Doris, and half a grand on my tab at the Five Spot, and $1,500 to a herkimer-jerkimer named Norman Schwandt to cover my losses on a particularly disastrous game of high-stakes Scrabble when Mr. Schwandt, a complete imbecile, pulled the word *zygote* out of his butt.

Paying off my debts would leave $21,000 for me. (No need to involve the IRS in the deal.) I was tempted to walk away with the dough and make a new start somewhere. Like Alaska, for example. Alaska is a top destination for fugitives. Rotgut sinners fly to Alaska and become Sunday school teachers; certified lunatics go into public service. Or I could return to the Upper West Side and find a sub-sublet and get a job at the Thalia selling popcorn and look forward to the next Richard Widmark Film Festival.

No, I said to myself, drawing myself up to my full six feet, one-and-one-half inches, I shall stay and do battle with Mr. Larry. Pure avarice is what drew me into the fray. Having an envelope fat with cash makes a man long to have even fatter envelopes. Whole bricks of crisp hundred-dollar bills packed into crates, a cool million in each crate, a row of crates stacked head high. Money, money, money, money, money. So I peeled off five hundreds and laid them on the bar on the way out. "Thanks for the tab," I said. And pulled off another hundred — "That's for you, pal." Jimmy held it up to the light. "Thanks," he said. "Anytime." He blinked. Me paying my bar tab: a historic moment. "You working for the dame?" I nodded. "You need an assistant?" he said. I shook my head. He poured a finger of twenty-year-old single-malt called Old No. 69 into a glass and pushed it at me. "On the house." A whiskey like Scotland herself, cloudy, bitter, judgmental, an aftertaste like chemotherapy. I held it in my hand to warm it and let the gravel and peat fragments settle. I took a sip and felt a great heat in the back of my mouth. Another burst of memory.

Sugar O'Toole and a summer night in Duluth and the taste of her kisses after we'd swum in Lake Superior near the iron ore discharge. But that's another story.

# 5
## WAITING FOR MR. LARRY

I hustled back to the Acme and stashed the tapeworm queens in my file cabinet, the Q-T drawer, and tucked the cell-phone/pepper-gas gizmo into a manila envelope marked STAMP COLLECTION: AVOID DAMPNESS. The wad of hundreds I clung to for a few minutes, fanning them, patting them, brushing them against my lips, my cheeks. What crispness and delicacy in a hundred-dollar bill that is fresh and uncrumpled. It breathes of possibility as plastic never can. Down below in the alimentary canal, my tenants were making themselves comfortable. In the Brew Ha Ha on my way in, I had picked up a cinnamon roll the size of a softball, and I could feel their excitement when it came tumbling down the chute. Fifteen minutes later I was still hungry. I ordered a pizza from Papa Rossi, a large pepperoni, extra cheese, and devoured that, and still was hungry, so I picked up a quart of spumoni and some macaroons and scarfed that up, went home, weighed myself, and I was two pounds lighter.

I handed Doris the $2,000 I owed her, and of course she lit into me. A simple "Thank you very much" would've been beyond her. "What am I supposed to do with this? Where'd you swipe this? Off a blind newsboy? Are the bills marked? Why can't you write a check? You expect me to go deposit this in the bank? As if I've got nothing else to do! And now I suppose you're expecting me to write you a receipt!! My God, what a day." She's a great complainer, that Doris, and also she likes to have you in hock to her and in her clutches. She stuffed the bills into her purse. "Oh, by the way," she said. "A guy named Larry B. Larry came around for you."

"What'd he say?"

"Oh, and now I'm your secretary????" She shook her head as if it were all too much for words, getting a wad of cash and being asked a simple question. "He said he's going to come back and hammer some sense into you. He wanted to go up and wait for you in your room, and I told him no. He had a friend with him, a skinny fellow, gray-haired. Suit-and-tie guy. Gynecologist named Buddy."

"Thanks for not letting him stay around."

"A gynecologist, Mr. Noir! What — you get some girl in trouble?" Then she looked me over up close. "If so, it must've been at gunpoint," she said. "So — you're up for first-degree rape. Just promise me this. When the cops come, don't make them knock the door down, okay? Give yourself up. Plead the Fifth and hope you get a decent public defender. I hope the girl wasn't underage. If so, don't expect me to be a character witness. No way."

"Doris, there was no rape and these are not cops. These are hoodlums and they don't knock doors down. They riddle them with bullet holes in a fusillade of hot lead, and afterward there's a funeral at which women in black mantillas weep into their hankies that they pull from their bosoms."

"I don't have a black mantilla, and I don't have a bosom either. Thought you would've noticed by now."

I shooed her away and flopped down on my bed. I wasn't in the mood to meet the enemy yet. I needed a strategy. I thought maybe Joey could be useful if I needed some muscle, or maybe Joey Junior. He is 437 pounds and has Percheron legs and a neck like a concrete block. He is a mild-mannered fellow, but if you leaned him up against a

Larry B. Larry and told him to shimmy, he could do some real damage.

I was writing Joey a note — "Thank you for paying me a nice visit to collect money for St. Bernard's School, which I know is dear to your heart. I am enclosing a check for $500 and hope this helps with the new gymnasium" — counting on his dementia to have wiped the slate clean, when a guy in a hideous green plaid jacket and eyebrows the size of laboratory mice walked in. The scuff marks on his wingtips and the flecks of what appeared to be tofu on his shirt-front, plus the slight indentation in his right index finger where a pencil rested when he wrote up the check, told me he was a waiter in a natural foods restaurant. But he turned out to be my accountant, Marvin Hansom, making a surprise visit.

"To what do I owe the honor?" I said.

"Your checking account is a black hole, Guy. It's antimatter. Don't touch it, or you're liable to wind up in a six-by-seven-foot cell with a hard bunk and a toilet with no seat."

"I'm on the gravy train, Marvin. I'm flush. Riding high."

"You're on the graveyard train. Your total assets are about enough to get you to Moline, Illinois."

73

"I'm on the verge of turning the corner."

"It isn't a corner, it's a cliff. And you went over it a long time ago. Sorry to be the bearer of bad news. But you're broke. Plus which, you owe me two hundred bucks. Guy, the handwriting is on the wall. The fickle finger of fate has written. Fini. Caput. Time to find yourself a paying job, maybe something in Housewares."

So I reached into my inside jacket pocket and withdrew the hundreds, and he fingered it, intrigued, I could tell. An accountant and all, with his rational biases and his numerology, and yet here was a wad of cash. "How did you glom onto this?" he inquired.

"As it happens, a fabulous opportunity has fallen in my capacious lap, and I've become a partner in a plan to sell a weight-loss drug that the American people have been waiting for."

"Aha," he said. I could hear the sprockets turning in his brain, the cogs meshing, the bevel gear turning the worm wheel. "Do you have a contract on paper, signed and notarized?"

I chuckled. "I am in partnership with someone whom I trust implicitly. I've taken a dose of the meds myself and lost three pounds in the past three hours despite stuffing myself with animal fats. If this drug works the way I think it will, I'm going to be enormously rich and moving up into a lower tax bracket."

He wanted to tell me I was wrong, wrong, wrong, but he was also considering what might be in it for him. His 10 percent fee for managing my 2 percent of a successful weight-loss drug might be enough to buy him the divorce he longed for and a diamond ring for the receptionist he adored, a big strapping girl named Chantal Smythe whom he met in a chat room called Married but Still Looking and took out on a date that lasted for seventy-two hours, most of it spent in a motel frequented by accountants called Cyrano's, in a room with a vibrating bed and a Jacuzzi with a mirror on the ceiling overhead surrounded by a string of pink Christmas bulbs. A private eye knows these things.

"I am done with the snoop business, Marvin my man. And if you want to be on my team, you have to do more than add up numbers."

He looked at me and blinked.

"You're going to have to poke your finger in people's chests and yell in their faces."

"Yell at women?"

"All kinds. I may need an agent. A go-between. A mouthpiece."

I'd just gotten a text message from a woman who needed somebody to yell at her, and to me it was proof positive that the time had come to retire from the field of private investigation.

She texted as follows:

It's like this, Mr. Noir. The man in my Adult Bible Study Group with whom I was having an affair decided he was gay and ran away with my husband, and our dog Godfrey went with them. I knew that the pizza delivery boy had a crush on me, and so we started fooling around, though he is 19 and I am 51. But he is mature for his age. One night Joe (my husband) returned to pick up his camping gear, and he and the delivery boy, Matt, who is not well disposed toward gays, got into a shoving match, and Orv (Joe's lover, formerly my lover) came after Matt, and I threw a toaster at him, and the neighbors came over, and their dog went after Godfrey, and the cops arrived and told us all to shut up. It was just one thing after another. My pastor Thorstein heard the whole story (we live in a small town) and was surprisingly sympathetic and not judgmental at all. He told me not to worry about it, that everything would be okay. I said, "Are you kidding? I feel terrible. Lives have been blighted, innocent people hurt, and it's my fault. I committed adultery." He said, "It happens all the time." I said, "What kind of a lousy pastor are you? Ever hear of the Ten Commandments?" He said, "We're all about mercy and forgiveness." I said, "What about contrition?" He was so smug, I just plain lost my temper and whacked him upside the head with a ballpeen hammer and ran him off, and that was the night the church burned down. I don't think I set it afire, but I can't be sure. I have been known to walk in my sleep. And the next morning when I awoke, I smelled of smoke. What should I do? Sincerely, Nora

In a rash moment, I texted back to her:

Darling, I'm driving to Montana to take up trout farming and don't expect to be solving any more cases for a while, not even ones as interesting as yours, due to a fondness for Scotch, thus the decision to relocate to a state where drunk driving is considered a normal part of life. But if you would be interested in exploring a romantic relationship, I am 65, weigh 220 pounds (lie, closer to 238), am 6 foot 1 1/2, have green eyes and thinning gray hair, and enjoy skating along the edge of mortal danger, which, judging by your letter, you do, too. I'm no spring chicken, but what I lack in agility, I make up for in skill and enthusiasm. Do not be fooled by the dry tone of this missive. I am a tiger. Be in touch. Xoxox Guy Noir

"Why I wrote that, Marvin, I can't tell you, but now she's sending me mash notes and sighing into my voice mail. I need management. Someone who will yell at me when I get off the beam." He promised to think it over and I paid him his $200 and he left to go see Chantal.

# 6
## A TEMPTING OFFER

Naomi was a hard worker. In two weeks, she wrote a memoir, *Why I Tried To Kill a Man, How I Went Free, Why I Would Do It Again,* which, at the urging of her publisher, she turned into a novel, *The Bright Side of Homicide,* which came out in April and shot to the top of the *New York Times* best-seller list thanks in part to the cover, a photograph of her that when you tilted it to and fro, she jiggled and shook her hips and licked her lower lip. I caught her late one night on C-SPAN explaining that violence is only a way of recontextualizing contradictions and creating a new trajectory in the allegory of good and evil. The guy interviewer seemed stunned to hear the word "allegory" from a dame with such beautiful bazooms. The book earned her a truckload of money, plus the cash flow from tapeworm sales must have been considerable, because a steady series of lovely checks dropped through the mail slot of Suite 1235, Acme Building, drawn on the Chase Manhattan Bank and payable to me, for $50,000 apiece, which I endorsed and dropped off at First National, where Charlene the cashier grinned — "You sure have an eye for those ponies, Mr. Noir!" — and counted me out ten hundreds, and off I went, happy as a mutt with a fresh porterhouse, and stopped at the Five Spot for a celebratory martini. Jimmy held the hundred-dollar bill up to the light and said, "You got yourself one damn fine printing press, Guy. Looks almost real to me." I dropped in at Candyland and bought five pounds of pecan turtles for the Sisters of Mercy and swung by Mariucci's Steakhouse, and old John showed me to a corner table under the big pictures of him in his Chicago Black Hawk days and punched me in the shoulder and brought me the usual — giant shrimp cocktail, sixteen-ounce New York strip, rare, twice-baked potato with sour cream, apple pie with cheese, and a Rusty Nail for the road.

"How do you do it?" he said. "Live the high life and still keep your boyish figure?"

"Plenty of sleep and plenty of exercise, John. I sleep with all the women I can, and we exercise together."

He grinned and we bumped fists, and off

I toddled into the night, rich and — if the glances of beautiful women were any indication — attractive, and both with so little effort on my part. I had scraped along for years, keeping my head above water, and now, no sweat, I was airborne. I bought clothes in smaller and smaller sizes. Old suits went off to Goodwill, and I switched over to jeans, black T-shirt, and herringbone jacket. I considered madras shorts, but my legs have weird hair patterns that look as if I reached puberty near a nuclear power plant. So I stuck with jeans, the expensive ones, French labels, prefaded in Provence.

I started exercising. I hired a personal trainer, Rochelle, who had me doing crunches and push-ups and lunges and taking long brisk walks as she held a stopwatch. She drove me hard. She'd been an army drill instructor, and abuse was her stock in trade. "Step up the pace, pork pie!" she yelled. "I want to see those love handles jiggle, want to see the dewlaps *bounce*, piglet! Go, go, go!" I loved her. I worked harder and harder to impress her. She yelled, "Jump, babykins! Hop and skip and then drop to the ground and give your mama a hundred crunches and fifty cherry pickers. Go, fat boy! Let's see you sweat!"

I stopped trying to finesse my bald spot with a combover and I shaved my head and started wearing dark glasses and using a powerful cologne called SOB, and suddenly I was like a prime rib at a piranha picnic. Women hit on me without shame. A seminarian named Cecily walked up at the Ha Ha and said, "You turn me on, mister." I pointed to the Bible under her arm. "Muzzle not the ox that treadeth out the corn," she said.

"What does that mean?"

"Come to my condo and I'll show you."

It is peculiar, being an object of sexual hunger for younger women and also knowing that a Larry B. Larry is gunning for you. Love and death in the same room, each one raising the drama of the other.

I met a lissome young photographer named Zuzu — she strode over to me in the Ha Ha and said, "I want to know you." And said she wanted to shoot pictures of me. "You don't mind posing in the nude, do you?" She got right to the point. She was tall and blond, except she'd dyed the roots brunette, an original touch. She put her hand on mine and invited me to come to her studio in the Rossmor Building and shoot a few and see what happens — "Na-

kedness can be tasteful, don't you think?"
And I looked out the window to see my
enemy slouching nearby in a soiled trench
coat, and he leered at me. And she said,
"And afterward we can sit and have a glass
of Pernod."

She went on ahead to turn up the thermo-
stat, and I headed for the Beethoven to
check on Louie Louey, and I climbed up
over a ridge of snow on the corner of Ninth
and Robert, and someone behind me chuckled, which distracted me, and I slipped, and
had it not been for my training in the tango,
I might've dislocated a disk and entered the
Dark Valley of Therapy in a nursing facility,
where Larry B. Larry would find me, helpless, an easy target for his devious schemes,
but I kept my balance, and the adrenaline
hit the worms in my gut like an electric
charge. They started dancing like the Rock-
ettes. I ducked into Danny's Deli, looking
both ways to make sure I was not being fol-
lowed, and ordered a pastrami on rye to
quiet them down, and before Danny could
mention my tab, I thrust five hundred dollars at him and then another hundred —
"Thanks for your support, pal." He got tears
in his eyes. "I had forgotten all about that,"
he said. "Friends don't owe me nothing.
Your friendship is what's of value to me, my

man. Appreciate it, though." And he tucked the dough into his apron pocket.

"Larry B. Larry was in here asking about you," he said. "Came in five minutes ago. You just missed him."

"And I hope to go on missing him."

He stacked about a pound of pastrami onto the rye and injected mustard and sliced it diagonally and gave me a cream soda on the house, and just the smell of pastrami got the worms excited. I sat down in the corner, where I could observe the front door. I took a big bite and fed the tenants, and a guy at the table behind me tapped me on the shoulder and said, "You mind not chewing so loud? It sounds like a horse eating oats."

He was a little guy with no chin and hound dog eyes, bald on top with a fringe around the roof, red vest, white pants. He looked like the director of a kazoo band. "No need to make a big production of it," he said.

"He put a couple leaves of lettuce in the pastrami and a raw onion. You want I should remove them?"

"Maybe take smaller bites. Maybe chew with your mouth shut. It sounds like you're eating a sheet of plywood."

"When did you start instructing other

84

people how to eat their food, mister?" And I took a huge bite and leaned toward him and chewed it, *splonch-splonch-splonch,* with my mouth wide open — childish, I know.

"Two can play that game," he said, and pulled out an apple and chomped it, horse-like, showing me his big incisors. And then my cell phone rang. It was a 612 number on the caller ID. I answered, and a nasal voice said, "Guy. Been looking all over. Thought you mighta skipped town."

"Why would I be skipping town, Larry?"

" 'Cause you know I'm looking for you, that's why."

"Where are you?" I says.

"Where are *you,* Guy?"

"Minneapolis. Sitting in the Forum Cafeteria on Seventh Street across from Dayton's, enjoying the excellent goulash."

"Nice try, pal." I felt a hand on my shoulder. A hostile hand. And turned, and there he was, snapping his cell phone shut, decked out in a dark blue gabardine suit, red polka-dot hanky in the breast pocket, pink striped shirt and green bowtie, a snap-brim fedora, tassel shoes, lavender socks. "Mr. Larry," I said, "you've been out shopping, I see. You're looking very spiffy."

He pulled up a chair and sat down. He plucked a toothpick out of his pocket and chewed on it thoughtfully and leaned forward and said, "Let me give you some advice, Guy. You got two choices here, one of them good, the other not so good. Naomi has filled your head with all sorts of sugarplum fantasies about Never-Never Land, but take a moment if you will and look around you. You're in St. Paul, Minnesota. You're sixty-five. Your gross income last year was less than what they pay the ladies in the grade-school cafeteria. Busboys earn more than you. These are facts. And let me give you another fact. The Food and Drug Administration is not gonna let you sell tapeworms in medicinal form to the American public. Naomi Fallopian wants to sell them retail in upscale men's clothing stores. Ain't gonna happen. The FDA is about to land on you with both feet. *Hard.* They're gonna throw a fine at you that'll clean you out for years to come and top that with three years in Sandstone prison. Not a happy prospect. The mattresses are hard plastic, the food is starchy, and every day a screw sticks his hand up your hinder. Your social life is limited to men with chronic depression and the girls in the picture magazines. That's where Naomi is leading you, pal. She hates men. Read her books. She's lured you out on a limb, and now she's gonna saw it off. She'll take the dough and flitter off to Switzerland with some male model in skinny jeans and leave you to pay the piper."

I was half done with the pastrami sand-wich and my worms were happy. I gave Wendell the counterman the high sign and said, "Coffee with cream." The worms tended to get twitchy on coffee. Cream might lessen the shock of caffeine.

"Your alternative, as I see it," said Mr. Larry, "is to let me and my guys take the worms off your hands and come up with another business plan that gets around the FDA, like maybe selling the stuff via the Internet and shipping it out of Jamaica. Anyway, that's our problem. If you turn over the goods now, we'll pay you exactly the same as she's paying you, not a penny less. In cash. You'll never hear from us, never meet with us — zero involvement on your part. If, God forbid, there's a criminal conspiracy indictment, you're out of the loop."

I waved to Wendell. "Another pastrami sandwich. And mashed potatoes."

Mr. Larry handed me a manila envelope containing a sixteen-page complaint of statutory purloinment of research on behalf of Dr. Buddy Wooden and naming me as a co-defendant. "Haven't filed it and hope I won't have to," he said, "but it'll fill you in on the details. Interesting reading." He was about to walk away and then turned back and asked me if I'd ever heard of the Bogus Brothers.

I had, of course, but I feigned ignorance. They were three bullies, originally from Bowlus, who walked around itching to sock someone in the jaw. Professional bouncers who worked clubs like Hook & Ladder, the Blowhole, Fresh Meat, and the No Holds Bar.

"We've paid them a retainer as possible consultants in the case," he said. "Hope we don't need them, but they're there if we do." He smiled a weaselish smile and said, "No rush. I've got all the time in the world. Have a good day," and ankled out, toothpick in his mouth, whistling "Please Don't Talk About Me When I'm Gone."

# 7
# WRESTLING WITH
# DARK ANGELS

I sat at my desk watching a big hairy spider rappelling down from the ceiling, and steered her toward the volume of Emily Dickinson's *Selected Poems,* which I keep on my desk as a magnet to attract sensitive women should I ever meet one. The book was opened to "Because I could not stop for death, he kindly stopped for me," and the hapless arachnid landed there near the word *immortality,* and I snapped the book shut. If you are going to wind up a splotch, why not in the margin of a work of art?

I knew I should've told Mr. Larry, "Hell no, what kind of a louse do you take me for?" and laughed in his face and I had not done that. It didn't even occur to me. So that is the kind of louse I am. The very one he took me for. A wavering friend. A lucrative offer to betray a pal does not always bring out the best in a man, I am sorry to say. I was afraid he might be right, that the cards were stacked and I was a sacrificial goat in the whole deal and Naomi was planning to throw me to the dogs of the FDA. I tried to banish the thought and it kept popping back up.

I woke up in the middle of the night, and a small insistent voice was telling me, "She is playing you like a fifteen-dollar concertina, and if the FDA comes around, she will leave you high and dry. Take his money and head for Key West. What is freedom worth, anyway?"

I tried to arouse my conscience by watching Bill Moyers on TV, and reading a Gideon Bible I'd stolen from a hotel room, and by walking around in a Lutheran neighborhood of south Minneapolis, but all I could think was — "Call Larry and turn over the worms, and you get a bucket of money and you stay out of prison. *What part of that do you not like?*" He had planted the seed of suspicion in my ear, and though I knew it was bad, nonetheless it stuck in there, and I could imagine the feds at my door, submachine guns in hand, and Naomi fleeing with Mr. Beautiful to a chalet in the Swiss Alps and me taking the rap and spending eight to ten years fending off the advances of desperate old cons.

All I had to do was pick up a phone and

call. Larry B. Larry had given me all five of his phone numbers: home, office, cell, car phone, fax.

I checked my horoscope for the day, which said: "You are a child of the universe, no less than the trees and the stars, and you have a right to be here." No help there.

*Well,* I thought, *if you intend to betray someone, at least you should call them up and tell them personally.* I called her over and over. No answer. Her voice mail was full, unable to accept new messages.

Naomi was gone. She had launched Elongate and gotten rich, and what did she need me for? Zero. She was a successful author — it wouldn't hurt her much if she lost those spare queens in my file drawer.

"But it would hurt you," said my conscience in a loud clear voice. "One thing you've always admired about the Midwest is the prevalence of trust. People count on each other here."

"Oh, go soak your head," says me.

"It's true," said the conscience. "Your pig farmer, for example. A truck pulls up to the pen, and the farmer herds a truckload of pigs off to be slaughtered. He doesn't count them or weigh them. He may not know the truck driver, but he gives him a check to cover transportation, and the driver goes off with the livestock. Pure trust. A handshake and a wave. A week or two later, he gets a check from the buyer, whoever that may be. No IDs are checked, no bonds posted, no ten-page contract signed and notarized. This is a culture where a person is trusted unless he proves untrustworthy. When you cheat, you are vandalizing something beautiful."

"Bad example," says me. "I'm the pig being loaded on the truck, and I'm trusting the driver to take me to an amusement park to ride the Tilt-A-Whirl and instead a guy is going to fire a bolt into my forehead and slit my piggy throat." I sat in my office, staring at the telephone, telling myself *Do it. Call L.B.* as my fingers walked toward the keypad, and then they walked away, and then my iPhone dinged, and it was a text message from Naomi.

Darling, I know it's unfair, leaving you to guard the chicken coop against the coyotes while I am gallivanting around Dallas, with Santa Fe, San Francisco, Seattle, Atlantic City, Cincinnati, Atlanta, Los Angeles, Las Vegas, Lake Tahoe, Omaha, St. Louis, Honolulu, Houston yet to go, and let me tell you: it's unfair and I love it. When your book is number one, you don't ever have to eat out of vending machines. You are cosseted and cared for, driven around in Lincoln Town Cars with leather seats by polite young men in uniform who leap to open the back door for you, you are housed in boutique hotels with French names, and whisked up in small private elevators to suites with real paintings on the walls, suites right out of Hotel Beautiful magazine, where English matrons in starched linen uniforms run you a hot bath and an hour later a Jamaican gentleman in black tie and tails serves you a Sauvignon Blanc and morsels of Sevruga caviar on quail's eggs on toast points, while a girl named Simone fluffs your hair and paints your nails, and Ingrid your masseuse is kneading your shoulders, and your personal pianist Phillipe is rendering your favorite Gershwin, and Ariadne your aromatherapist is spritzing you with narcissus, sassafras, and cinnamon. Darling, I can never go back to the squalor of academia, the dusty offices, the dreary classrooms reeking of indifference, the horrors of the cafeteria. Nor can I return to Minnesota where everyone is expected to suffer and if you don't, they will see to it that you do. I am much much too happy. Meanwhile, our little business enterprise is going like a house afire, mon amour. Fabulous word of mouth, sales exploding daily, and guess what? The filmmaker Michael Moore has lost 100 pounds on the pill, and now he has a workout video of himself in bikini briefs doing exercises to old labor songs. It's called Solidarity Aerobics. Isn't that cute? I'm on a book tour for a couple months, soaking up the critical acclaim and the phenomenal sales numbers, but I miss you desperately. There is a guy missing from my life and it is you, darling. Do keep the second week of June free, and let's drive north to Lake of the Woods, where my cousin Will has a cabin on a heavily wooded island that is not within sight of any other island. A one-bedroom cabin with a commodious bed and a sauna just big enough for two, and I think we could make a memorable weekend.

I checked my calendar, and the second week of June was completely free. As were the first, third, and fourth. And that was that. The prospect of sitting naked with Naomi was what moved me to call up Mr. Larry and say, "No deal. Forget it. Ixnay.

No can do."

"Okay," he said. "Then I will inform the Bogus Brothers that they should find you and provide additional motivation."

"Do what you're going to do, and just know that I have friends who are armed and demented and too old to care what happens to them — they don't want to spend their declining years in a herd of wheelchairs in a nursing home. They would rather go down in a blaze of hot lead." And I hung up.

# 8
## THE MALE SITS ON THE NEST

Spring comes suddenly in Minnesota. You're holed up in your dank cave, living on Spam and canned water chestnuts, reading the obituary pages, your prostate feels like a hockey puck, you light a candle, you curse the darkness, and the drummer you were marching to is leading you into a vast frozen swamp. You are out of cash because detective work is slow in the winter: it's so cold you can't tail anybody because nobody goes anyplace because if they did, they'd freeze their tail off, which in this case would be you. So they don't, and you don't either. You just sit at a desk trying to visualize success, and instead you see a moonscape of suffering. It's like trying to build self-confidence by reading the prophet Jeremiah, and no wonder you feel like a shrunken plant trying to grow in the dark. You see a gray cloud low in the sky, which looks like someone you once knew, and then realize you are looking at the reflection of your own face. It isn't a cloud, it's you, Bubba. You long for sunshine, vegetation, warmth. You call up Danny's Deli to order a life-saving hot pastrami and you get an old lady on the line, and you ask for Danny or Wendell, and she screeches at you, "Wrong number, creep!" and now you hear *All Things Considered* in the background, and she yells, "Get out of my life or I'll come over and cut your throat with a serrated bread knife!" and you're shocked to realize you've reached a public radio listener, probably a public radio *member,* maybe a birdwatcher and book club member, who nonetheless has murder in her heart, and you realize how thin is our veneer of civilization, and if a blizzard hit and supermarkets ran low on food, this woman might shoot you for the last jar of pimento olives even if she does listen to Bach and Mahler — she'd bury a knife in your chest for the last chunk of Cheshire cheese. This realization pushes you to the brink of despair. Visions of liberal Unitarian women, veterans of civil rights and ERA marches, turned into raging animals. And then suddenly it's spring — you look out the window one morning, and a girl so beautiful she makes garage doors fly open walks by in a bright green skirt and sweater

— no parka, no scarf or mittens — and a breeze blows her skirt up over her shoulders revealing that she forgot to wear underwear — *and she isn't embarrassed in the least!* — and two days later the tundra blossoms and burgeons and foliates, and flowers leap from the ground, and Minnesota becomes so lush and verdant, you could almost film a deodorant commercial here.

Larry B. Larry fired off an ultimatum: *Surrender the queens in forty-eight hours or accept the consequences.* I opened the Q-T file drawer and opened the bag, and there they were, eleven of them, hatching eggs like crazy. I called Ishimoto on the cell and told him to come to my office. "Is the office secure? No Boguses?" he said. He came right over, a tiny Japanese man in black Spandex, shaved head, dark glasses, a silver canister under his arm. He walked in, and before I could say good morning, he said, "Lock the door, Mistah Cholly." And went around pulling the shades. I tried to engage him in conversation, but he waved it off. I opened the drawer, and he scooped out the eggs with a spoon. And he said: "Did she tell you we must store the eggs in you?"
*Pardon me?*
"Eggs need to be kept in warm place. You

are the host, Cholly."

He opened a black leather bag and brought out six little plastic balls about the size of walnuts but soft, and he pointed to my mouth and traced a line down my gullet to my belly. "Eggs safest in there."

"I signed up to be security. I didn't agree to be a mule."

He didn't understand. So he whipped out a cell phone and punched the number one, and there was Naomi. *Why does Ishimoto have instant access to her while I have to leave messages on voice mail? Oh well.*

"Darling!!!" she cried.

"Where are you??" I replied.

"Bengali, on a trolley." The publicity tour was taking her around the world (Sun Valley, Mount Denali, Bali, Sea of Galilee), the book was an international hit, published on the subcontinent under the title *Pruning God's Garden,* and Indian women, long oppressed, sold into marriage, abused, enslaved, were buying it by the carload. Naomi was number one in New Delhi and on her way to Shanghai and having a whee of a time, eating up a storm, keeping trim thanks to Irma and Herman, her personal parasites. "I have missed you, darling Guy. The book is setting sales records left and right. But fame is ephemeral and money is only a means to an end, and it dawns on me now that long-term loving relationships are what matter most in life."

"When do you come back?"

She wasn't sure. With Mr. Larry and the Bogus Brothers gunning for her, she thought maybe she should cool it on the other side of the world. "Ishimoto sent me pictures. Three gorillas with shaved heads and spiderweb tattoos and pecs the size of pot roasts. Darling one, life in Academe did not prepare me to fight off illiterate brutes, only highly educated ones. Not the kind who want to sock you in the puss. So I'm counting on you to guard the nest."

"I don't know, sweetheart. I've been going through some physical changes lately, and I'm feeling punier and punier."

"Of course! The tapeworms are working! You're becoming svelte, darling. A slender stripling. I can't wait to see for myself and feel your abs, your delts and pecs."

"Perhaps I could fly to Bengali and reconnoiter," I said. "I almost forget what you look like. We could recline under a banyan tree and read aloud from the *Kama Sutra* — I understand there's a chapter called 'Plumbing the Inner Sanctum.' "

"Oh darling. If only. My heart leaps at the thought. But I need you *there*. In St. Paul.

Fighting the good fight. Protecting our flank."

The word *flank* brought up visions of her pale radiant haunch in the spotlight of the Kit Kat Klub as she unsnapped the G-string and twirled it over her head and it flew like a glittering bird into the mitts of the howling mob.

"That's why we're sending you those lovely checks," she murmured. "I notice you keep cashing them."

"Perhaps we could afford to hire additional security," I offered. "Beefier men in their twenties with jujitsu skills. I don't lean on people quite so well as when I was bulkier."

"The fewer people in on the secret, the better," she said. "You're lighter and quicker, and you're wilier. You can't stomp on these Boguses, but you can outwit them." Easy to say when you're lying around the Ganges Hilton and a guy named Gupta is bringing you a tall mango smoothie. "And now Mr. Ishimoto is scared to death. He got an anonymous e-mail saying 'We know what you're doing, and we know where you are. Hand over the livestock. Or else.' He is having a double hernia over it. So we need to store the eggs in a warm moist place. And I thought immediately of you."

When she said "warm moist place," I felt all warm and moist and trembly all of a sudden. I tried to say "No way," but the words wouldn't come out of my mouth.

"Ishimoto will put the eggs into little soft shells, and you swallow them like pills. They're harmless. They stay in your tummy until it's time to retrieve them, and then you take a mild laxative and out they come, warm and moist and ready to be put in pills."

She was breathing into the phone, and it was such tender breathing. Purring. A sensuous sighing, or susurration, like the wind in the silvery cottonwoods by a burbling brook flowing through the whispering prairie grasses by a long two-track dirt road somewhere in Nebraska, not that I've been there myself but I read Willa Cather once when I was dating an English major named Leslye who was, in fact, from Lincoln, Nebraska, and I believe "susurration" was the word Willa used.

"Are you sure the eggs won't hatch and I'll be eaten up by ravenous worms like that emperor in the Bible?" I murmured.

"No, no, no, no, no," she said. "No chance of that."

"My tapeworms won't kill them?"

"No, no, no." And then she said she would

do anything for me — I believe a trip to Tuscany was mentioned, and an oceangoing yacht, lunch at the White House, VIP tickets to concerts, health benefits, retiling a bathroom, a pony named Muffin — "Stand tall, darling Guy, and guard the bulwarks and I will make you so happy your heart will turn cartwheels. When you and I are sunbathing on the deck of our yacht anchored in the Aegean off the island of Patmos, sharing a wineskin of retsina and figs wrapped in grape leaves, and we dive off the stern deep into the clear water and embrace in the depths of the ancient sea where Helen of Troy, who was fathered by Zeus in the form of a swan, was abducted by Paris and therewith launched the Trojan war, and O my Guy, you will be glad you did faithful service for our company," she murmured. My lips were twitching, my forehead was warm and moist. I said yes. How could you say no to a long, lingering underwater embrace in memory of Helen of Troy? Sometimes life is like that. You're looking for dimes, and it tosses you diamonds.

Mr. Ishimoto shoveled eggs into the walnuts and sealed them with a soldering iron and handed them to me. Six of them.

"I'm not sure I can swallow these," I said.

"These are not what the average person would consider small. They are objects of some size. A person could choke to death."

"They compress, Mistah Cholly. They are swallowable."

I was about to argue the point, and he popped one pod into my mouth and shoved it past the point of no return, and down it went. "See? No problem."

He kept popping them in, one after the other, and poking them in past my tonsils. It felt like I was swallowing golf balls. I could feel them all the way down the gullet and into my gut.

"Excellent job, Mistah Boss!" he cried. Hard as it was to swallow them, it was worse to imagine them coming back up. Or what it would feel like when they shot out the other end. I hyperventilated a little and put a paper bag over my head and thought of the Aegean and Naomi naked with bubbles streaming from her mouth as she kissed me in the azure depths.

That evening the Bogus boys attacked Ishimoto's laboratory in Robbinsdale and rampaged around, busting down doors, while Mr. Ishimoto lay trembling among the ductwork in the crawl space overhead. They threw petri dishes and fish tanks and mold specimens to the floor, ripped up hoses and wiring, and pulverized his notes, and when they found no worms or eggs, they flew into a towering rage and jumped up and down and screamed like banshees, and eventually the cops arrived, three squad cars and a chopper, and chased the boys over the bushes and down a median strip and across a church parking lot and through a child-infested mall, where the Boguses gave them the slip, and meanwhile I drove out to comfort him. He was sweeping up the debris and grinned when he saw me and patted my stomach. "Treasure chest," he said. "You take good care, Cholly." He had spoken to Naomi. He held up five fingers. She had offered him 5 percent of the net for his efforts. I slapped him on the shoulder. "Hey, that's great. You deserve it," I said, insincerely.

I tried not to feel bitter. When the total is up in the millions, a guy ought to be happy with 2 percent, especially when he's been scraping bottom for years, but I couldn't help but be a little resentful. I was the one carrying the eggs, not the Jap. I was the one Larry B. Larry was threatening. I made a mental note to myself: *Talk to Naomi and negotiate a contract, and don't just accept the first offer like a spineless jellyfish. You're a*

*New Yorker, not a Minnesotan, so say what you want in clear English. Be bold. Don't underbid yourself. But first, maybe it'd be good to face up to the Boguses as a proof of your loyalty. Tussle with them and get Naomi's attention, and maybe then she'll raise your share to 5 percent or even 7 or 8. The bigger they are, the harder they fall.* Danny at the deli had told me an interesting fact about the Boys. Their names were Tony, Tiny, and Ronnie, and they were former pro rasslers, under the ring names Devastation, Destruction, and Death, and were terrified of spiders, snakes, and bats. "All you got to do is put something on them that crawls up them and they turn to jelly." A big, hairy spider would do the trick. I had plenty of those in the office. So what's to worry about?

# 9
# THE BOGUS BROTHERS ATTACK

As I got skinnier, I got great pleasure out of swanning through a crowded room and leaning against a pillar or abutment and striking an elegant pose and watching women fling themselves at me like moths on a lightbulb. On May Day, a child of twenty-one named Moxie hit on me in the Brew Ha Ha. She was plump, like a popover, and wore daisies in her hair and a smock that said *Color Me Happy,* and she said, "I'm sitting over there and I'm going, like, Who is that totally hot guy? And I'm, like, Do I dare walk over and talk to him? And I'm going, No way. And then I'm going, like, Why not. You look hot. Like, how old are you?"

"Darling child, if you and I were to talk and my shoulder brushed your shoulder, we'd be caught in a rushing torrent of ravenous passion and down the white-frothed spillway and over the roaring cataract of romance and into a whirling vortex of desire — kissing, caressing, clutching, grabbing, thrusting, crying out with hunger and delight — and, beautiful as our intentions might be, it simply wouldn't work and here's why — I live in many different verb tenses, such as the imperfect indicative, the past imperfect, and the subjunctive, and you, sweetheart, only in the present indicative. I mean, you're going, like, Who is that guy? but I have gone or might have gone or will have gone, but you just pretty much keep going, and someday you may look back and wonder where I went. And I'll be, like, not there."

She gave me a triumphal smile. "I had been hoping you could come to my apartment and we might have come to know each other better," she said, a predicate that almost stole my heart away.

I might have kissed her then and there, but a scrawny kid with black horn-rims walked up. Black T-shirt, black pants, black tennies, hair dyed black and sitting lopsided on his head. "Where you going with this old dude?" he said to her.

"He's chill, Tony."

"Chill? You mean like, cold. Like in, laid out on a marble slab. Don't mess with him unless you know about resuscitation, Mox."

And he lunged at me and took a swing and missed and fell down and banged his noggin on the table and knocked himself silly. His nose was bleeding all over the black shirt. He drew himself up tall and glared at me and dabbed at the blood with napkins and finally came up with a good exit line. "Watch yourself," he said to me. And exited.

"How about it? Want to come with?" she said to me.

"I'm going, like, I don't think so. But thanks for the offer." She was very nice, as they say, but too young. I don't get into bed with a woman who might, casually, in the post-coital glow, ask what the sixties were like. Not my sixties or the other one.

Oddly, now that I didn't need to work a lick, I got a stream of job offers. The phone jingled like a Salvation Army Santa Claus.

1. Lost dachshund, tan with tattoo of rosebud on left ear, answers to name "Rigatoni," belonging to Desdemona and Jonah the Shoshone duo-trombonists from Sedona, Arizona, who perform pro bono with their palomino Corona and Rigatoni in a kimono.

2. Woman needed to know if a couple she'd

invited for dinner that night were Republicans so she should seat them away from her husband, who is still livid about George W. Bush and gets all flushed and talks about war crimes and saliva flies out of his mouth.

3. Woman wanted me to drive to Decorah, Iowa, to spy on her daughter at Luther College to ascertain if she was getting enough sleep and who is the man she hears clearing his throat in the background when she calls Lori in the morning.

4. A young guy with long, backswept hair swept into my office, black cape swirling around him and clouds of cologne — a tenor from Minnesota Opera. "They try to kill me! The director. *Direttore.* He wants acting, not just singing! *Realismo.* Wrestle the soprano to the floor and roll around. Some sopranos roll better than others. Okay, I do this. Now I'm Rodolfo in *La Bohème.* Artist in the garret. Snow falling. He makes the stage so cold I can't sing *Che gelida manina.* I am too *gelido.* Like *gelato. Terribile! Non è possibile. Idioto! Stupido!* And Mimi is skinny. String bean. *Fagiolo verde.* Nothing to grab hold of." He wanted me to follow the opera

director home after rehearsal and hold a knife to his throat and yell, *"Questa è la fine. Morte à te, un traditore."* (This is the end. Death to you, treacherous one.)

5. A woman wanted me to locate a lesbian couple she saw two minutes before on West Seventh Street walking into Cossetta's who she was sure she used to know but she'd forgotten their names — one woman was wearing a yellow nylon jacket that said GACK! on it, and the other was in black tights and a tanktop — and what if she ran into them again?

6. A man called and asked for a huckleberry pie. "This is Guy Noir, P.I., not Guy Noir Pies," I said, having gotten calls of this nature in the past. "Then how about banana cream?" he said. "I'm a private investigator, sir." "Great. How about you go track down a pie for me, then?"

7. A man wanted me to go to Gary's House of Hair on West Larpenteur and pick up a toupee for him — he was too embarrassed to do it himself. Black, not too long on the sides.

8. A woman called who had finally finished

reading *Moby-Dick* after ten years and had forgotten what the book was about, and could I help?

9. Plus the usual lost car keys and misplaced glasses. The umbrella forgotten in a bar called Michael's or Mitchell's that used to be on Ford Parkway, then went somewhere else, maybe shelling.

Marvin had told me, "Get it in writing," and I left a message on Naomi's voice mail, asking when we might discuss some sort of formal agreement — that I was happy with a handshake blah blah blah but I had some big cases in the works, Microsoft, Google, Bloomberg, Apple — lie lie lie — and my staff was pushing me to regularize the arrangement — and just then I heard big steel-toed boots in the hall and the growl of industrial-strength testosterone and my name shouted and a big fist banged on the door. "Open up, or we'll bust your thumbs!" somebody yelled. Somebody who sounded quite capable of thumb-busting. And he had colleagues. I heard them muttering, *Gumba-gumbagumbagumba.*

"Put a hanky over your face — we're fumigating with cyanide!" I yelled, and made a hissy sound through the keyhole.

That stopped them for a moment. Gave me time to open up the Q-T drawer and take the bag of queens and deposit it into a White Owl cigar box and set it out on the desk, in the open. Sometimes Obvious is your best strategy. And I grabbed the spider out of Emily Dickinson and held it up as the gentlemen in the hall hit the door with their shoulders — once, twice — and *krrrrrrackkkk* busted it off the hinges and *kerwhammo* it smacked flat on the floor, and three big bruisers in black leather landed hard chins-first, and the concussion dazed them long enough for me to jump over the line of scrimmage and hustle out and down the stairs to the tenth floor and dart into the fern-infested offices of Bergquist, Batten, Bicker, Buttress & Bark, past a stunning young receptionist who whinnied as I dashed through, knocking over a big yellow vase that I neatly caught one-handed and carried through a door marked private and through a room with a shiny mahogany table as long as a canoe and floor-to-ceiling shelves packed with red leather-bound legal tomes and into Birch Bergquist's office — she sat with her back to me, talking on the phone — and crawled under her desk. "Excuse me," she said into the phone. She poked me with the toe of her sling-back pump. "What is going on here?" I was panting like a bull moose in heat. "Mr. Noir! Stop looking up my skirt!" she said.

She was right. I *was* looking up her skirt. Pure reflex. Pale peach undies, if you must know.

"I'm trying to prevent a homicide," I said. "My own."

There was male bellowing out in the hall, a sort of *rar-rar-rar-rar,* like a chainsaw idling. Large men blinded by rage, hyperventilating, stamping their big hooves, all hot to find something to pummel.

"Let's step into the conference room," she said. So we did. It was ten steps away, a long room painted a soft beige that reminded me of the lower back of a woman I used to know. And there, at the head of the table, sat the very woman herself, Sugar O'Toole, my ex-lover, like a Celtic goddess, her hair dyed a rather convincing shade of auburn, her eyes cerulean blue — and that's from a guy who doesn't even know what *cerulean* means. She wore a long black skirt and a green V-neck T-shirt that, when I looked down the V, my mind was flooded with beautiful memories.

"Oh, Guy!" she sighed. "I am so glad to see you! I've been dreaming about you."

"Sugar! What are you doing here?" She

leaped to her feet and got me in a clinch and breathed on my neck and cried real tears. Six years I hadn't heard from the woman — she didn't write, she didn't call, she didn't text — and now she clung to me like I was a flotation device. Six years ago I was roadkill. Carrion. And now I was Cary Grant.

"I came here to work out a separation from Wally," she said.

"What's wrong? I thought you two were happy as could be."

"He's a very nice person, Guy. He makes a lovely four-cheese omelet, and he does laundry and even folds the clothes, and he cleans bathrooms with a passion. But two weeks ago he came home and announced that he's decided he's a woman. He's wearing green plaid skirts and knee-high stockings, and the hormone treatments have given him bigger breasts than mine. He's Wanda now and apparently content with his lot in life, thanks to a caring therapist and powerful drugs, so I'm working out the separation, and Birch tells me I'm walking away with a cool million, and that's not so bad except I'm lonely as a hoot owl. Wally left my bed a year ago, back when he started getting really, really interested in window treatments. The only emotional support he needs is from his shih tzu Poo-Poo. I'm desperate to find a partner. Or whatever you call someone you sleep with. I'm not getting any younger, you know. I hold the banister when I descend stairs. I read the obituaries with real interest. I attended three memorial services last month alone. I no longer know the names of famous celebrities. My chin is starting to jiggle when I walk."

"Your chin was never your best feature where I was concerned," I said. "I much preferred your br— your brain."

"My brain is wobbling too," she said. "I keep forgetting where I put the car keys." Her voice got quiet. "I miss you, babes. I can't tell you how good you look to me right now." She gave me a full frontal squeeze, and I remembered all over again how much I prefer the small-breasted woman. An enormous prow may be attractive to a nursing infant, but to me it's only a barrier. You want to nestle up to a woman, but those enormous buttresses are hard to get around.

I stroked her slender freckled arm. "I miss you too, but at the moment I'm on the run from three guys who want to rip out my entire reproductive system."

The three gentlemen had gotten quiet out in the hall. Birch had gone out there and (I assumed) spoken to them and threatened them with a restraining order or something. Sugar kissed me full on the lips and inserted her tongue. Tentatively, but still. She wanted to meet me for a drink. "Please," she said. "What do you have to lose?"

"My life, for one thing. These guys are on the rampage, Sugar. I'm in mortal danger. I have something they're willing to kill for."

"Let's slip out the back way, darling. My car is parked just down the alley. I'll take you over to Minneapolis. My apartment on Washington Avenue. They'll never know. Wally's gone to a Home & Garden show. It'll be just you and me and the dog. Oh, darling —" And she put her tongue in my mouth again and caressed my wisdom teeth, which has always been a turn-on for me, in case you're interested. Also my earlobes and my left nipple. The right one, not so much, but if you so much as brush against the left one, I will leap into your arms and beg for mercy.

I pushed her away, but gently. "Sugar, you and I have broken up so many times, my heart jingles when I walk. I have no capacity to love. Especially not now, when I am about to have the stuffing knocked out of me. Fear of imminent death pretty much stifles a man's sex drive, it's been shown over and over. Men facing a firing squad do not produce erections to the same extent as men in a luxury hotel room with a king-size bed."

Birch came back in the room and grabbed my arm: "I told the goons you went up to the roof to jump, and they went off howling for you. Let's get out of here."

Sugar was still clinging to me. "My car is close by — I'll bring it around to the front."

"Bring it around to the back," said Birch. "I'll send him down to George's office, off the loading dock." And she towed me out, through her office and past the stunning receptionist, whose name, I saw, was Autumn, which, I was about to tell her, is my favorite of all the seasons — the goldenness of it, the urgency of beauty, the crispness of the air — but Birch had a tight grip on my wrist, and out into the hallway we went — the rank odor of testosterone in the air — and down a narrow hallway to the freight elevator, in which, she told me, her less savory clients, the heinous ones, molesters and such, rode to and from her office.

"Go down to George's, the janitor — you know where it is — just off the loading dock. He's a decent guy. He can watch for Sugar to pull up. Be careful."

"If I'm never seen again alive, tell Naomi

that her love for me was the best thing that ever happened to me. The best."

She nodded. "Go," she said.

"I don't have an up-to-date will, so my assets I'd like to divide between Jimmy the bartender at the Five Spot, and Wendell the counterman at Danny's Deli, and my nephew Douglas, the union agitator."

She said she would take care of everything.

The freight elevator came up, and I got on board and pressed B, and down I went, ancient chains clanking in the shaft above like Marley's ghost. There were two battered file cabinets riding along, the files of Dr. C. L. Sheck, Psychiatry & Neurology, a mass of human suffering described on paper on its way to an incinerator, the old man newly retired to Montreal with a twenty-four-year-old dancer named Shirelle. He was a bow-legged, barrel-chested, bald-headed monkey with a giant schnozz and a spade beard and black horn-rim glasses whom I once consulted about my personal sorrows, and after ten minutes he said, "A man who can't get laid in St. Paul, can't get laid." Uncooked vegetables, he told me, are the secret of virility. He never sent me a bill.

The elevator clanked down to the basement and landed with a hard thump, and I hustled back into George's dim cave of an office. An impressive mountain range of junk rose from the desk, and an old dinette set with a TV on it, tuned to the Handyman's Channel on cable. The camera was focused on a wall covered with wet paint, and it didn't move. And there in an ancient recliner lay George, grizzled, bundled up in his old DeLaSalle letter jacket, reading a paperback, *Compassionate Custodianship*.

"Hey, Noir, how's it going?" he growled. "Something wrong with the radiators again? That cheapskate Lou won't let me call the plumbers."

I was staring at the TV. The picture didn't move. Live coverage of a wall covered with wet paint.

"Birch sent me down. I need to hang out here for a few minutes until Sugar picks me up."

He roused himself and cleared away some paper plates with pizza crusts on them and asked if I wanted to play cribbage. "Sure," I said, and it was a shock to me, after he dealt the cards, that I'd forgotten the gist of the game. I guess fear will do that to a man. I could feel my tenants trembling in my gut; probably they could taste my fear. Visions of large men stomping on me and driving enormous fists into the tapeworms' living quarters.

"You seem uneasy, Mr. Noir."

"Terrified is more like it, George."

"Is there something you'd like to talk about?"

"George, you're a janitor, not a therapist. So don't talk like one."

"You don't have to be a therapist to care about your fellow man, Guy."

George is a squatty man with two days' growth of whiskers and big tufts of ear hair and warty hands, not a person you'd care to discuss your innermost feelings with. I told him to care about some other fellow man and leave me out of it.

"What kind of attitude is that?" he said. "You're lonely. Just say so. Loneliness is a form of suppressed rage. I've seen a lot of it in men our age."

"I'm not your age, George. Nowhere near your age."

He grabbed my wrist. "I'm only trying to help — and I'm not going to stop caring just because you're in denial." I tried to take my wrist back, and the old booger clamped down on me like a dog on a sirloin.

"You need me, and you don't dare admit it!" he cried, leaning up close, breathing his onion breath on me. "Have you ever heard of Joseph Campbell and *The Trail to Ecstasy?* We're all on a quest to escape the feminine wound and be initiated into manhood and harmonize our duality in the great circle of the universal soul. Plain as the nose on your face. You're broken inside and so am I. We can help make each other whole." I tried to shove him away and he wouldn't let go of my wrist, so I kicked him, and he fell backward and banged his head on a steel locker, and when he got up, a little woozy, he knocked over a pile of old paint cans, and suddenly there was bellowing from down the hall and the *rar-rar-rar-rar* of the three brutes like hounds on the trail of an escaped inmate.

"George," I said, "I wasn't here, and you didn't see me. Okay?" And I took a deep breath and climbed into a packing case a moment before the *rar-rar-rar-rar* came thundering into the office.

"Hey numb nuts," said a low growly voice. "You seen a heavyset guy in a blue suit come by?"

George shrugged. "Not recently."

"Well, if you see him, tell him that we are on his trail, and if he doesn't come out of that box right now, we're going to pick it up and heave it into the Mississippi River."

I climbed out as gracefully as I could under the circumstances. "Gentlemen," I said. "To what do I owe the pleasure?"

# 10

## IN THE CLUTCHES
## OF THE EVIL THREE

The Bogus Brothers were XXX-large, about a sixty-four long, I'd say, solid muscle, with legs like tree stumps. Shaved heads, big eyebrows, flared nostrils, a lot of facial scar tissue, as if they'd been pounding fence posts with their foreheads, muscle shirts under the black leather jackets, and purple warm-up pants, and they smelled like old gym socks sprayed with cheap cologne. They wasted no time in chitchat. They grabbed me, one to an arm, and the third guy held my necktie, and they perp-walked me out back into the alley, the broken glass crinching underfoot. An old cat let out a meow like fingernails on a blackboard. Steam hissed from a manhole. The smell of burning rubber and lost hopes.

"Listen," I said, "I have promises to keep and miles to go before I sleep. I left my horse in the woods beside a frozen lake. Where it's snowing downy flakes."

They said not a word, not even a syllable. I told them a whole string of humorous jokes — about lost lithographs ("Someday my prints will come") and wet newspapers in an entryway ("These are the *Times* that dry men's soles") and a rooster sicced on Margaret Thatcher by a man who just wanted to see a chicken catch a Tory — but they didn't laugh. "Tell us where we find the worms," said the guy holding my tie. "You know which ones. The ones with the eggs."

"Do worms lay eggs?" I said. "I thought chickens did."

He flexed his right arm, and the bicep filled up his jacket sleeve, and he drew it back to drive it into my solar plexus, and just then a horn honked, and up drove Sugar O'Toole in a black BMW. She rolled down the window and said, "Which one of you fairies thinks he can leg-wrestle a skinny little progressive Democrat?"

That amused them. The Bogus boy holding my right arm relaxed his grip and chuckled and said, "Take your pick, lady."

She got out. She had changed into a loose low-cut blouse of a translucent fabric and a short skirt that drew your eye toward what, in some circles, is referred to as the "money-maker" — she was quite a sight as she stepped around the front of her car, her arms folded ninjalike, looking straight at the big boys, unflinching.

"I've been doing leg lifts and built up my glutes to where I can sit down naked on a bench and pick up a quarter with my cheeks. Want to see me do it?" She smiled. "It'll cost you a quarter."

The boy holding my left arm suddenly dropped it. His mouth was open and out came a sort of a *huh-huh-huh-huh* like a car trying to start on a cold morning. I reckoned he was laughing, but he hadn't had much practice, so it sounded rather painful.

"Or we can arm wrestle. I'm a black belt in tai chi, and I've been working out with unabridged dictionaries — one kick, and I'll lay you out like tenpins and collect your nuts with a letter opener and donate them to a museum."

"Let's see you do it then," said the Bogus holding my right arm.

"You want to go first?" she said.

"Sure. Why not?"

"I'll give you a choice: a flying kick to the jaw, or I'll tit-slap you until you beg for mercy."

Sugar's breasts are not big enough to slap a Chihuahua. The Bogus boys glanced at her chest and chuckled heartily.

Something about a beautiful woman brings out the John Wayne in me. I said, "Come on, you sissies. Afraid she might hurt you?" The boy with the flexed bicep told me to shut my yap, and he hauled off to slug me, and Sugar yelled, "Hey!" and he turned, and she had three syringes in her left hand. She hurled them at the Bogus boys, *thump thump thump,* hard and with great accuracy, and hit them in the shoulders, right about where the school nurse gave you your measles shot, and the needles stuck, and the brutes went pale from fear of needles and their legs turned to rubber, and they took a wobbly step or two and sank to the pavement and lay in a heap, mouths open, eyes rolling, drooling, out like a light.

"You okay?" she said, and grinned. I nodded. "Get in the car." She poked a Bogus with her toe, and he murmured something like "Can I open my presents now, Mama?"

"They're going to be miffed when they come to," I said.

She got behind the wheel, and the BMW eased down the alley and out onto East Seventh. "It's an animal tranquilizer. Got 'em from a naturalist friend who uses them to bring down moose so he can install radio transmitters in them," she said.

And we looked at each other and said,

"Hey!" at the same time. And she made a quick U-turn and drove back up the alley.

We debated whether to put the tiny transmitter in a Bogus boy's underarm or in his buttock, and in the end she inserted it into his scrotum. "Easier to numb," she said. "One little incision, and in it goes." She was right. She snipped the sack, slipped in the transmitter, which was about the size of a penlight battery, stapled three stitches, sprayed antiseptic, and that was it. Easy. She drove away and whipped out her iPhone and pressed the Map icon, and up came the grid of St. Paul and a flashing blue bulb marking the spot where the Bogus boy lay with a radio in his nuts.

It kept flashing as we drove to Minneapolis and around the university campus and along the Mississippi past the dam and the Stone Arch Bridge and old flour mills and Grain Belt beer sign and over the river and through blocks of old warehouses that had been turned into art galleries and lofts and chichi restaurants, and it was flashing in the same exact spot when we arrived at the old *Minneapolis Journal* printing plant, now a six-story condominium complex, and walked into her living room full of leather furniture and a big glass-topped coffee table with enormous picture books of Picasso,

Peru, petroglyphs, and the pool halls of Pittsburgh, Pennsylvania.

I could hear a dog growling in the next room. "That's Luke. Wally wanted a guard dog. At first we named him Mark, but when we called his name, he'd go pee on a tree. So we changed it to Luke." The dog sounded like he took his job seriously.

"He's tied up. Don't worry." She sat me down with a glass of Pernod and disappeared into the bedroom, and when she came back, she wore black capri pants so tight I could make out George Washington's face on the quarter in her pocket. And she had on a blouse made of thin netting; it had less fabric in it than you'd find in the average doily. She moved across the room with the grace of a cat, and if I was the sparrow, well, there are worse things than dying at the hands of a beautiful predator. She said, "I've never forgotten how good the good times were, Guy. There will never be anyone for me like you."

"What happened with Wally? Why did he decide to be a woman?"

"He went on a big fishing trip to Alaska. A plane flew him into a wilderness lake, and he stayed there alone, in a tent, for seven days, and it rained the whole seven days, and his only reading matter was *Vogue* and

128

the *Ladies' Home Journal* and he just decided he should try a different gender, that manhood hadn't really worked out for him. I wish him well. I think everybody deserves to be happy. And I think the change will be good for him. The man hasn't read a book since he left the ninth grade. No movies, no newspapers. Fishing was his world, and Green Bay Packer football. From August through February, the man watched every Packer game there was to watch, twice. Taped the games for replay. Bought highlight videos. Had a big TV over our bed, another in the kitchen, one in the bathroom. Wore a Packer jersey and helmet. He was having headaches and went to a shrink, who told him that football was his way of destroying all the estrogen in his body, and Wally went cold turkey, and sure enough, the shrink was right. The holidays and the Super Bowl rolled around, and Wally turned the TVs to the wall and donned a green and red apron and did a fabulous Christmas, constructed a lovely mantelpiece, decorated a ten-foot spruce with real candles, roasted a goose which was scrumptious, baked a mince pie, played carols on a soprano recorder, everything. Centerpieces made from old egg cartons, hand-frosted windows, hundreds of cookies. The man had found himself. And he had no more interest in sex with me. He looked at me like a cat looks at a dog. And that's when I started dreaming of getting back with you. Remember when we danced on that barge on the Mississippi, you in a black tux and me in nothing at all? We jumped on at the Ford locks and rode upstream and I danced in the towboat spotlight and the pilot said to take it off and I did and we got out at the St. Anthony lock and you put your jacket on me and your billfold was gone and we got a ride with the boy with the missing arm who loved Hank Williams so much?"

Well, what could I say?

# 11
## SUGAR REUNION

It was a wild romantic evening with tumultuous tumbling and rolling and exclaiming, quoting from poems, crying out extravagant sentiments, the giving of directions, moaning. When two grown-up people know what they want, they don't waste time discussing politics and the ups and downs of the real estate market. She grabbed my hand and led me up the stairs and bedroomward, and I kicked off my shoes and unbuttoned my shirt, and she tore off my pants, the old pants with the belt pulled up to the fourth notch. "Whose big balloon pants are these?" she cried. "You working in the circus now??" It was nice of her to notice my newly gained slimness, or at least slimmerness. She threw me into bed and flung her undies to the wind, and I held her close and kissed her freckled shoulders and collarbone, which I had yearned for for six years, and also her slender arms and girlish navel and firm belly, and we got right down to business, and it was all rather thrilling and luxurious and ecstatic except for the heaviness in my gut. We jumped around in bed and tried out various interesting little things from Sex 101, and Sugar was crying out "Yes! Do that! Do that!" Meanwhile those little plastic capsules were bouncing around, and my worms were pitching a fit, and then I got an overpowering urge to head for the toilet. Egg capsules were making their way into the colon and pressing against the sphincter. Ishimoto had never mentioned anything about this. I did not want them to come blasting out during a paroxysm of rapturous delight.

It is practically impossible for a man to maintain an attitude of wild passion when he feels the urge to take a crap. "What's the matter?" she said. I said, "Darling, gotta pee. Be right back. Hold that thought." And trotted off to the toilet and tried to move my bowels but nothing was moving. There was a painful traffic jam in there, and I thought of picking up the toiletside phone and dialing 911 and letting the EMTs work it out, and just then a large animal hurtled itself against the bathroom door, barking like a jackhammer. A German shepherd, I guessed, but I didn't ask for his passport.

And in about three seconds, six plastic capsules came shooting out of me and floated in the toilet like buoys in a swimming pool. The dog was clawing at the door and snarling like I was out to get his girlfriend. I could hear bare feet on the stairs. I fished out the capsules and dropped them into one of Sugar's nylons hanging on the shower curtain rod and stashed it behind the clothes hamper.

"Lukie Luke! What are you *doing?* Shame on you." She tapped on the door. "It's okay, darling. He won't bite."

And indeed he did not. Though he did grind his teeth and give me homicidal looks. She led me back up the stairs. Why I found this erotically stimulating, I can't explain. Survival is a turn-on, I guess. We jumped back in bed and made love until my head was spinning like cherries on a slot machine, and Sugar in her ecstasy sang the Minnesota Rouser — *"Rah Rah Rah for Ski-U-Mah, Rah for the U of M"* — and fell back and lay fully spent, curled up on her side, and I pulled the blanket up to her chin, and she murmured, "You're the best, Guy. The absolute best." And was asleep.

I tiptoed down to the toilet, and the dog poked his head up from the couch where he was dozing. I retrieved the capsules and washed them off several times with soap and warm water and — Lord have mercy — swallowed them, gagging on each one, but down the chute they went. I spotted Sugar's cell phone on the coffee table and picked it up. The dog's eyes were locked on me like airport radar. The blue light was flashing on the same spot in downtown St. Paul. Evidently the Bogus Brothers had spent four hours snoozing in the alley behind the Acme. I could imagine their vast rage when they awoke. They would be in a mood to wreak devastation. Maybe I had better purchase a few dozen of those wildlife syringes and learn to throw them with accuracy. I tiptoed up to the bedroom and slipped into bed beside her, and she turned in her sleep and sighed at the proximity of me and nestled close and put her little curly head against my shoulder and smiled. And a few hours later I awoke to the smell of espresso and fresh-baked croissants.

I got out of bed and walked slowly naked into the bathroom, aware of her eyes feasting on me. I never would've done that back in my fatso phase, not slowly. I'd have grabbed a towel or something to cover my big butt. Now it was skinnier. Shapely, almost. She climbed into the shower with me and soaped my back and I soaped hers

134

and she soaped me some more and then we writhed together under the hot water, all slippery and soapy, and dried each other off with enormous fluffy towels.

And then we did other things.

And afterward I lay, scratch marks on my back, my hard drive tingling with bliss, Sugar in my arms, feeding me a croissant stuffed with blackberry jam and a perfectly poached quail's egg on a triangle of brioche. And felt the urge to get dressed and get out of there. *What was wrong with me?*

"You just get younger and younger," she said. "Move in with me, Guy. It'll be just like it used to be, except better. I've got a million in the bank, and the apartment is all mine. We'll throw away the fish lithographs and make it our little love nest. The best is yet to be. My heart is a caged animal, Guy, and you hold the key in your hand."

There was a barely audible growl from the corner and a grinding of teeth. You didn't have to be fluent in German to know what he was saying: "You move in here, and your troubles have just begun."

"We'll make a happy life together," she said, her pale green nightie draped loosely on her naked body, her cheek pressed against mine. "We'll go to the movies, we'll cook together and read poetry aloud, and we'll dance in the dark and do wonderful impulsive things like dropping everything and flying to Montana just because we want to, and walking up a mountain trail in the summer rain and singing Neil Young songs. That was the problem before, Guy. We weren't impulsive. We were cautious. We dated for six years, and I can count the number of crazy impulsive things we did on one hand. But look at you now. You're elegant. Dashing. A new Guy. I always begged you to lose weight, and now you have, darling. Oh Guy, you're the handsomest, sexiest man in Minnesota. And probably other states as well. Marry me."

And the dog said, "Go ahead, try it, and you'll wake up one morning with one less testicle."

The thought of singing "Heart of Gold" in a high voice in a public place did not appeal to me, nor did reading poetry aloud. "The Cremation of Sam McGee," okay, and maybe some Robert Frost, but most poetry requires you to go limp with awestruck wonder at stuff like dew on the grass, and clouds in the sky or deer in the underbrush. Sorry, but I'm not a fourteen-year-old girl.

And then I remembered Naomi, the yacht on the Aegean, the underwater kiss. Women possess an infallible rival detector. If you so much as peck another woman on the cheek, your Primary Woman can sense this and she will hunt the peckee down and remember her scent and monitor your movements ever after. It was only a matter of time before Sugar said, "Tell me about you and Naomi Fallopian. Are you sleeping with her? Have you ever, or are you hoping to in the future?" And Naomi would phone in from Phoenicia: "So what's this I hear about you and that O'Toole woman?" If Naomi and Sugar found out about each other, they would drop me simultaneously, and I'd be suddenly loveless and penniless and pathetic.

It wasn't easy to tear myself away. Sugar begged me to stay for lunch. "Scallops, my love, on a bed of basmati rice. And then you, my love, on a bed of silk and satin." I had to lie and say that Larry B. Larry was meeting me at the office in an hour. She wanted to drive me to St. Paul. "No, no, darling, I want to keep you out of this." The truth was, I needed to be alone and think. A man loves wild passionate sex, and then he would like to be solo for a while in an undisclosed location. Maybe climb a tree and sit on a high limb for a few hours. And look at the sky.

"Be careful," she said. She kissed me

good-bye (many times and many places), and I glanced down the front of her shirt at the two friendly puppies lying in their hammocks, and I promised to be in touch, and waltzed out the door and down to the corner where a taxi was parked and climbed in and said, "St. Paul. Downtown."

"You work around here?" the driver said. He was a big fellow. He filled up half the front seat. Balding, with a long thin braid hanging down.

"You could say that."

"Night shift, huh?"

"Sometimes. When I'm lucky."

"My girlfriend works a night shift at the hospital. We're saving up our money because in January her and me are having a baby."

"She and I," I said. "Not 'her and me' — 'She and I are having a baby.' "

He slammed on the brakes, and the cab skidded toward the curb, and a bus swerved around us, honking. "That's not funny," he said. "Where do you get off saying a thing like that?"

"I was correcting your grammar."

"And leave my grandma out of it, too, you jerk!"

"You said 'her and me are having a baby.' It's *she and I.* That's all."

"I ain't taking that from you —" And he

lunged over the front seat and grabbed my jacket and took a swing, and I managed to open the door and slide out, and he came galumping around and grabbed my shirt, and I had to hit him hard, an elbow to the ribs and a right jab to the chops, and he fell down and lay whimpering on the boulevard. I saw the roll of twenties in his shirt pocket, and I grabbed it. "I ought to charge you tuition," I said. "The College of Etiquette. You just learned why you ought to think before you lose your temper. A couple hundred bucks might make it more memorable. But I don't want your money —" and I stuck the roll in his mouth. "I just had sex with a fabulous lady and then a fine croissant as well, and I've got all the cash I want. But that doesn't change the fact that *'she and I'* are having a baby. Your girlfriend and I. And she told me that your sperm are weak swimmers, barely motile, and that's why I was brought into the case. Let me know when the baby comes, and I'll send a box of cigars." And I turned away and then turned back and said, "Last time I saw a mouth like yours, it had a hook in it," and walked fifty feet to the bus stop just as the express to St. Paul rolled up — no need to break into a trot — and boarded *and* (get this) *I had exact change in my right-hand pants pocket* and dropped in the six quarters and they played the first six notes of "Dinah" exactly as Thelonious Monk played it in his 1955 Blue Angel recording. Talk about smooth. Perfect timing. And then the nubile young woman I sat down across from looked up and smiled at me. She smiled and held the smile and was about to say, "Don't I know you?" and I was about to reply, "No, but give it time, darling, give it time." But before she could say it, the bus stopped, and she got up to get off and looked back at me with that *I-will-always-look-back-on-this-as-a-tragic-missed-opportunity* expression on her face. And I gave her a *Look-me-up-I'm-in-the-book* look. She got off, the door closed, and I farted. It sounded like Jack Teagarden's growly trombone in the second chorus of "I'm Coming, Virginia."

# 12
## GETTING LUCKY

So Sugar thought I was the handsomest, sexiest man in Minnesota. She who had often in the past addressed me as *"Lard Ass."* In general it had started to dawn on me that I was indeed becoming rather gorgeous. My size L shirts were billowy, and I was tucking in the tails, not leaving them hanging out as I had in my spare-tire days. The 38 waists were sagging on my hips — which now were bony, not humps of flab — so I switched to 36, a little snug but not for long, and by June I was a 34. My chins didn't wibble-wobble when I shook my head. Even my earlobes seemed skinnier. Women in coffee shops gave me the eye who had never eye-balled me before. Several women in their twenties flirted with me. Brazenly. Sidled up on the street and asked for directions to the Cathedral but in a way that suggested they'd be glad to skip the Cathedral and accompany me to a bar for a cool drink and some frank conversation. Soon I needed a belt to keep up the 34s and was looking at 32. I felt weaker, the worms made me queasy when they got jumpy. And ever so often I let some thunderous farts, big boomers that smelled like deceased penguins. But I was turning into a show horse. Definitely. I was in better shape than when I was seventeen and graduating from Ira R. Globerman High School on West End Avenue. Back then, thanks to high metabolism, I could pack away eleven hot dogs at a sitting, and now tapeworms gave me all the metabolism a man could want. I was doing forty sit-ups at one sitting and almost fitting into a 32-inch waist and wearing skimpy briefs to show off my tight glutes. Not bad for an old man.

My landlady, Doris, noticed my slenderness. She, who took a quasi-spousal interest in my comings and goings, said, "You're looking rather skinny, Mr. Noir, hope that doesn't mean you got some sort of wasting disease and one day we're going to detect a powerful stench and the cops have to break down your door and there you are on the floor in your skivvies and your body bloated and your glassy eyes staring up at me. It takes a long time to get the smell of a dead body out of an apartment, and even then they're hard to rent, so if you're about to croak, I'd rather you go out in the street and save me the headaches. Or when you sense the end is near you could dive off the High Bridge. You hit the water, it's as good as hitting concrete. How about it?"

I assured her that I had plenty of shelf life left, but she wasn't buying it.

"I've seen it before — there was a gentleman named Hobbs who tried to lose weight on a diet of bran flakes and mothball crystals. He played piano in the lobby of the Lowry Hotel and everything he played sounded like 'Till There Was You.' He got so fat he had to sit sideways at the keyboard and play one-handed, and one summer he lost about two hundred pounds real fast, went from pumpkin to string bean. Went off to work one day and was knocked down by a small child on a tricycle and hit his head on the pavement and couldn't remember 'Chopsticks' and had to go to work as a chicken plucker. This isn't some harebrained weight-loss scheme you bought from an ad in the back of *Field & Stream,* is it?"

"Just trying to take care of myself, like every other guy my age. The days of wine and roses have become the days of tea and rosehips. A sad story. I used to be Mr. Excitement, and now I'm Mr. Appropriate."

She studied me through narrowed eyes. "What is Elongate?" she said.

I feigned ignorance. "A long gate? Is this a joke?"

"Those pills you took. In the silver foil wrapper."

I had switched to new worms, since the old ones seemed to be slacking off, and like a dope I had put the wrapping in the garbage, which Doris studies like an archaeologist. The woman knew as much about me as if she were my wife.

"Those are vitamin E pills, Doris. They give me illusions of youth."

"Don't go taking some pills you bought off the Internet that they make in some tiny Caribbean island that contain God knows what. People have sent away for stuff like that and wound up losing a kidney."

"All's well, Doris. Don't give it another thought."

But I started to wonder: How much did Doris know? Had she listened to my voicemail messages from Naomi? Was she maybe in Larry B. Larry's pocket? Someone that cranky and abusive you assume is playing you straight, but anyone can be bought if you can meet their price.

My phone rang. There was a high-pitched tone at the other end. Someone's fax machine. I yelled, "Wrong number! I am not a fax machine!" Hung up. Two minutes later same thing. I whistled into the phone, hoping to confuse the circuit, and hung up. Two minutes later, *ring ring ring.* And *eeeeee eeeeeeeeeeeeeeeeeeeeeeeeeeeeeeeeeeeeeee eeeeeeeeeeeeeeeeeeeeeeeeeeeeeeeeeeeeeee eeeeeeeeeeeeeeeeeeeeeeeeeeeeeeeeeeeeee eeeee.* Technology! Nerds taking revenge for us not inviting them to our parties. So I had to trek on down to Bergquist, Batten, Bicker, Buttress & Bark and borrow *their* fax machine and haul it up to my office and plug the son of a gun in and receive the fax, which was, of course, a menu for a taco joint, Nacho Mama, and then haul the machine *back* to Bergquist, Batten, Bicker, Buttress & Bark, a huge inconvenience.

On the other hand, I did run into Birch Bergquist, who visibly brightened at the sight of me and said, "My God, you look great." A compliment from a gorgeous woman makes my whole day. It is better than finding a twenty-dollar bill behind the sofa cushion.

My plan was to slim down to a 28 while avoiding the Bogus Brothers and buy me a white linen suit and go away on a fourteen-day cruise of the Aegean aboard the *MS Bellissima.* I'd read the brochure. I could imagine lounging around on the afterdeck, tanning myself, surrounded by a bevy of sloe-eyed beauties in diaphanous dresses listening spellbound to my stories of detection and the darkness of the human heart. I had big plans. I'd travel around Italy while my eight-room apartment on Fifth Avenue overlooking Central Park was replastered and painted, the bedroom looking out at the treetops, the kitchen redone with Mexican tile floors and countertops, all described in a splashy story in Lifestyles of the Rich and Handsome. (GOTHAM'S MOST ELIGIBLE BACHELOR LAVISHES FORTUNE ON $4. 2 MIL PIED-À-TERRE), me in a silk running outfit, an attractive personal assistant named Deirdre pouring cream in my coffee.

Why not?

I believe in progress. Look at Barack Obama. The guy was a state legislator and then he wrote a fine book and gave a big speech, and suddenly people were excited about him running for president. And lo and behold, a black guy with an odd name beat a war hero. Usually the heavyweight beats the lightweight, but an ordinary horsefly has been known to drive an elephant crazy. *The Washington Post* did the same to Richard Nixon. The world turns. People demonstrated in the streets of Cairo and shouted "Down with Mubarak," and other people joined them, and the army refused to shoot them, and eventually the regime fell. Ditto Qaddafi. And look at Oxford. It started out as a shallow bend in a stream where herds of dumb cattle could be made to cross, and over the years it's become quite a prestigious university. We live by improvements. Bad luck can change. Redemption is within reach. For weeks, Joey Roast Beef wandered around unable to distinguish his left foot from his right hand, and then he went to a shrink who gave him a little pill and next day Joey sat down and wrote a poem. Joey, a poet! Who knew?

*This Is Just to Say*

I have taken the body
that was in the icebox
and which you were
probably saving for evidence.
Forgive me it smelled bad
So pale and so cold.

It just goes to show you never can tell. He was so pleased, he sat down to write another.

Let me not to the marriage of true minds

Admit informants. Love is not love
Which goes to the cops with what it finds.
A guy like that I'd have to remove.
Oh no, it goes straight for the mark
And posts a lookout for the break-in,
It is the car that's waiting in the dark
To race away after all the stuff is taken.

And then he quit taking the pills because
he felt so good and he stopped writing
poems and he got mad at me again. So
maybe it all evens out in the end.

# 13
## JOEY AGAIN

Joey Roast Beef liked me just fine all that spring and then in June I went back on his shit list. Senile dementia is funny that way. It comes and goes. He had forgotten what he was mad at me about, but he knew that something was stuck in his craw, so he buttonholed me in the Five Spot one sweet summer night — came beetling splay-footed along the bar, his jowls bouncing on his starched shirtfront and the red tie with the purple bacilli, and he jabbed a hairy finger in my sternum and said, "What gives, Guy? What's goin' on? Something is. You owe me money? You been badmouthing me, or what's happening? Fill me in."

"Joey, we had a disagreement about American foreign policy toward Canada, and you argued for patience and negotiation, and I argued that we ought to bomb their hockey rinks and show them we mean business, and now I see that you were right and I was wrong and we're pals again."

"You're lying. You tried to pull a fast one on me, and I was gonna pump you full of lead. I remember that much, ya crum bum."

I suggested we sit down and make peace over a fine Scotch. He shook his head "You're lying to me, Noir, I can see it in your shifty eyes. You think just because I'm eighty-two, you can sneak one past me. Well you can't." And he reached in for his shoulder holster and I had to restrain him.

"Don't have a coronary over it. You're a beautiful man, Joey. You've been like an uncle to me. Let me buy you a drink." And I waved to Jimmy. "Coupla Scotch and sodas! Ice on the side. And a boiled egg and some pickled pigs' feet."

Steam was coming out of Joey's ears. He was not to be pacified. He struggled to pull the gun out and called me vile names, and I was afraid he would shoot himself in the armpit. He spat a big gob in my face. "You're dead, Guy. I wash my hands of you. And don't expect me to speak at your memorial service. I am going to skip the whole thing and have a big lunch until after they put you in the ground, and then I'm gonna come over and piss on your grave. So I hope they bury you in a raincoat."

He was beyond reasoning with, so I shoved

his gun into the ice bin and ankled it on out the back and down the alley and into the back door of the old Visitation convent, now a fancy office complex, and into the elevator and up to the fifth floor and the former chapel that — miracle of miracles! — had been made over into the Minnesota Musical Theater and an audience was waiting for the curtain to open on *Two to Duluth* by my old flame Beatrice and her new love, the librettist John Jensen, she having ditched her husband Brett who suffered from memory loss and was busily writing things he'd written years before and that were not improved by the passage of time. I squeezed into a seat in the back row and hunkered down, but Beatrice spotted me and leaped up and galloped back and gave me a big showbiz hug. "Darling!" she cried. "It's been too long!" The boyfriend looked pretty much as you'd expect a John Jensen to look: pale, bony, wary, limp handshake, a look of chronic pain.

"If I had known you wanted to come, darling, I would've invited you!" Then she stepped back and gasped. "My gosh, you've lost weight. You look fabulous! I heard you were dating Naomi Fallopian. Congratulations! She and I go way back. I adore her book, *The Blessing of Less.* John and I want to make it into a musical. A one act."

"The blessing of what?"

"She hasn't told you? She's become very spiritual lately, and she's on an antimaterialism kick."

The lights dimmed, and she and the boyfriend tiptoed out the back door, and the curtain came up on a big photographic backdrop of Duluth, the Lift Bridge and all, and the little orchestra in the pit struck up the overture as a lady usher came by and motioned to her head, and I took my fedora off. "Thank you," she said.

The music was rather thin and whiny. Four large people in parkas came out and sang:

*When you are white*
*You are white all the time*
*You're very uptight*
*And you drink a white wine*

*When you are white*
*An average white man*
*You get a bright light*
*And work up a tan.*

*You can't hear the beat —*
*It's sheer frustration —*
*You've got two left feet*

*No syncopation,*
*'Cause you're Caucasian.*

I leaned back and started to doze off and then smelled an exotic perfume from overhead as Birch Bergquist stepped into the row and stood over me, her hair like melted caramel, her jeans so tight, I could read the embroidery on her underwear. It said *Tuesday.* She sat down next to me and pressed her body against mine. It was like the front bumper of a '57 Buick. Her heart was pounding like it wanted to get out. Or maybe it was my heart. "I spoke to Mr. Ishimoto today, Mr. Noir," she said. "Naomi's in terrible trouble. And I can't reach her. The Food and Drug Administration has assigned a man named Kress to hunt her down and throw her into prison. I've got to make sure she stays in Paris and doesn't go to Switzerland, where she could be extradited.

"I'm scared," she said, leaning her head on my shoulder. "Larry B. Larry and those thugs of his are rumbling around and one of the brutes is holding his crotch and bellowing your name. And Mr. Roast Beef is steaming mad. I ran into him in the alley, and he's furious because I won't tell him what's going on with you and Naomi. I told him it was lawyer-client confidentiality, and he told me he was going to change his policy of not hitting women."

"Baby," I said, "he's after me too, so maybe you and I ought to fly to Paris and start a new life together."

She looked me over. Back when I was a lummox, she wouldn't have given me five seconds, but now that I had a thirty-inch waist and a nicely defined jawline, she did not dismiss me out of hand. She considered the proposition for perhaps twenty or twenty-five seconds, and then she smiled and said, "Don't think I haven't thought about it, buster. You used to be a hulk and now you're a hunk, and I've been feasting my eyes on you for weeks now." And just then I smelled hair tonic, and it was Joey, all 340 pounds of him. He squeezed himself into the seat next to me, and I could feel the snub-nosed revolver in my ribs. Or it might've been a stapling gun, but I wasn't going to ask.

On stage, a man was singing to a Holstein cow:

*Moo a while, chew a while,*
*Regurgitate*
*I'll take a rag and wash your bag*
*And I will pump out fourteen gallons.*

*Go ahead and swish away that fly, baby,*
*I don't mind you dropping a cow pie,*
  *baby.*
*If your butterfat content is high, baby . . .*
*You can't give me anything but milk.*

The audience applauded like mad, and the curtain came down for intermission. Joey was not paying any attention to the play whatsoever. "Noir," he said, "you are the reason I am on Xanax, and now I remember why I'm mad at you. It's about you and that Naomi Fallopian and this whole tapeworm deal you got going, which you are trying to cut me out of, and if you're wondering why I'm gonna blow your brains out, that's your answer right there."

He sat there, beads of sweat on his forehead, wheezing, his landslide of a gut draped over his belt buckle: he looked like he could use a couple dozen tapeworms himself.

"Shortness of breath, Joey — you better see your cardiologist."

"It's just a cold," he said. And he cleared his throat and spat the phlegm into a hanky. It sounded like someone shoveling wet silage.

"Just ate lunch, huh, Joey? Cheese and onions. Thanks for sharing."

"What is that supposed to mean, wise guy?"

"It means you and I are friends and what's bad breath between friends, but if you're planning to go visit Lulu LaFollette, you might pick up a mint mouthwash at the drugstore."

"First I'm planning to blow your face off, and then I'll get me a mouthwash."

"How's Pookie, Joey? Is she better?"

"Who you talking about?"

"Pookie. P-o-o-k-i-e. Your kitty."

No light shone in the fat man's eyes. He was gone.

Birch started to say something about taking a deep breath and counting to twenty, and he told her to shut her pie hole. Meanwhile the audience headed for the coffee stand in the lobby. I offered to get Joey a latte, and he told me to shut up and not make a move. I could see Beatrice and her beau in the back of the room, receiving the compliments of their hoity-toity pals.

"Joey," I said, "we've got to get you into an anger management program of some sort. This has got to be awfully hard on your heart."

"I got a strong heart, Noir, and you broke it with your treacherous ways, and that's why I gotta get rough with you."

He drove his fist into my solar plexus, and all the air went out of me *whooof,* and none of it came back. My liver lit up with pain, my pancreas too, and there was a wetness in my trousers that hadn't been there a moment before. A flock of warblers circled my head, and church bells rang for vespers. I was looking over the rim of the Grand Canyon, and then I was holding onto a parasail as I drifted down toward the canyon floor, and then my mother was bringing me a birthday gift in a big red box. And then I was very nauseous.

"There's more where that came from, Noir. Tell me where I can find Miss Naomi Fallopian, because if you two are riding the gravy train, then I'm coming with. First-class. Lower berth." I wanted to say, "I know nothing about this, Joey," but I didn't have enough air in my lungs.

And then the lady usher returned. She had big white incisors and hair-colored hair, and from the shape of her, you could see that she was not a prisoner of Pilates. She leaned over Joey and said, "You can't bring a gun into the theater, sir."

"Oh yeah? Where does it say that, lady?" he barked. Well, she must've been a junior-high teacher at one time — she simply reached down and took the gun out of his hand and said, "I'll just hold on to this for a while, mister." He tried to argue, and she clapped a hand over his mouth. "You make me come back here again, I'm going to slap you so hard, your head will spin like a gyro." And she walked away.

Joey tried to rise, but that seat wasn't made for 340 pounds: the arms held him like a C-clamp around a Parker House roll. He tried three times to heave himself to his feet and couldn't budge an inch. He beseeched me to help him up. "Look. I only brought the gun to get your attention. I never woulda shot you. And I only hit you because it was all I could do since I couldn't shoot you. So give me a hand, and we'll call it even."

I patted him on the shoulder. "Enjoy the show, pal. Don't forget to clap at the end." Birch and I slipped out just as the crowd was filing back into the theater. Beatrice smiled at me — "Not sticking around?" I said I'd had an urgent call from a friend. "So you liked the first act?" I said I'd never seen anything like it. She managed to take that as a compliment, and Birch and I trotted out the door and around the block to the Five Spot.

She asked me if I was okay. "Could be worse," I said, drawing a shallow breath, the air trickling into my collapsed chest. Jimmy the bartender told me I looked like death on toast. I whispered, "Just had a little run-in with Mr. Roast Beef, thank you, and bring me a gin martini a.s.a.p. And a white wine for the lady." The wine came, and I could tell it wasn't dry enough for her, or complex enough, so she just sniffed it. I got some gin in me, and my solar plexus started to revive. "So," I said, "you were saying —"

She told me that Mr. Kress of the FDA had to be dealt with pronto, otherwise he would sink the ship and settle our hash, and some of us — she poked me — might wind up in the Big House making license plates. "You got your hand in the Elongate cookie jar, and the feds can snap that lid down on your wrist, and they'll perp-walk you into the courthouse, and Gene Williker will have a field day, baby. He'll refer to you as an 'aging gumshoe' and 'local Sherlock,' and he'll use an old photograph from your fatso days, pouches under your eyes, jowly, dog-tired, and he'll quote Lieutenant Mc-Cafferty at some length about your being a relic of the old St. Paul underworld, and moms and dads can now sleep better without the likes of you walking around, and all your friends are going to see this, and — don't kid yourself — friendship is a fragile thing. You see your old pal Guy Noir in handcuffs and read that he peddled pills that hatched tapeworms in people's bellies, and you turn away in disgust. Mr. Kress can do you real damage, Guy."

"So what's this I hear about Naomi writing another book?"

"Naomi is out there in Cloudland. Like a lot of enormously wealthy people, she's gotten all wrapped up in spirituality. She's about to go live in a yurt with some yahoo in a saffron gown and let him explore her inner being, if you get my drift. We've got to save her from herself."

I was shocked, naturally — Naomi had been telling me for months that she was in love with me and the ground I walked on. "Who's the yahoo?" I said.

"His name was Rosen, he was raised on a resin farm in Racine, but he's risen from Rosen and become Rama Lama Mononga-hela, and he's celibate, but I suppose that's up to her now, isn't it. Anyway, they live in her cottage in Southampton, but they're planning to move to Rawalpindi, and Naomi is weaving her *dhoti* on a hand-loom and chanting in Sanskrit, and she shucked her tapeworms, and she's gained forty pounds, which, how you can do that on a diet of lentils and chickpeas, I don't know, but she has. You wouldn't recognize her."

My adorable Naomi, transformed into a full-figured Hindu mama. As the kids would say, *Ack!*

"So how do I get in touch with this Kress?" I said.

"He contacted me through Larry B. Larry. You know him?"

"Larry B. Larry? I know him like a white rat knows a python. How'd he get hooked into this?"

"He's a friend of your ex-girlfriend Sugar O'Toole's husband Wally's boyhood chum Brett, who was married to Beatrice Olsen, the composer whose musical we just saw the first act of, until he found that his memory loss was cured by a well-bred brunette from Broken Umbrella, Nebraska, named Brenda Brickelle, a heart breaking beauty with big brown eyes, and Brett crossed that bridge and burned it behind him."

My head spun. A whole Russian novel's worth of complications in a hundred words or less. "But how did Beatrice find out about me and Naomi?"

"Beatrice's hairdresser is Naomi's treacherous half-sister Missy. Who happens to be dating Lieutenant McCafferty's son Sean, who plays shortstop on Sugar's masseur,

Sheldon's, softball team the Shoreview Sharks along with Beatrice's trash man, Trent. St. Paul is just one big small town, Guy. Everybody knows someone who is a friend of a person who knows you. It's not like Minneapolis. There are secrets in Minneapolis. For example, the fact that you jumped in between the sheets with Sugar — it happened in Minneapolis, and so nobody knows it."

"How do you know it?"

"I didn't. I was just guessing, and now you've confirmed it."

Birch turned away, and I saw a tiny iridescent tear form in her eye. "I hate to admit this, but — I'm jealous, Guy. I always thought that you and I would make a wonderful couple. I've been flirting outrageously with you ever since I don't know when. Been batting my eyelashes until the lids are sore. Wearing blouses with necklines down to my sternum. What do I have to do? Pull my skirt up over my head?"

I bought her a drier, more complicated wine, and she liked that more, and I tried to explain that the night with Sugar was a one-shot deal, a trip down Memory Lane, but women have a built-in lie detector when it comes to Other Women, and Birch wasn't buying it, and who could blame her? "I'm glad that you go to the trouble of lying to me," she said. "I take that as a compliment. It means I'm important in your life." She swigged the rest of her wine. "I see you and me in a cabin in the woods with a big wood-stove in the middle and a bed hanging from the rafters on chains, and I imagine us making that bed swing from side to side, night after night. But first I want you to get Mr. Kress off our backs. Otherwise, I'll be talking to you through two inches of Plexiglas, baby." And she stood up, and out the door she went.

I loved the sight of her rear end sashaying out of the bar. It spoke a language all its own. It said, "I am yours soon as you do the work, and the sooner the better." On the jukebox, Amy Miami was singing,

*Why do I keep trying when I know the score?*
*You will leave me as you have before.*
*But I love you, my beautiful one.*
*Oh there is nothing new, nothing under the sun.*

# 14
## MAKING MY MOVE

I don't ever attend church. If you saw me in church, sorry, but that was someone else, not me. I don't go. For one thing, organ music reminds me of creepy movies about deformed people. And for another, the sermons just get dumber and dumber. Priests used to address the subject of sin, and now, for fear of offending the sensitive, they mostly talk goodness and mercy, and if they talk about sin, they come at it from the wrong direction — "Alas, alas that man is capable of such despicable things!" — whereas the private eye accepts that the despicable thing *was* done and asks, "Why was this done and by whom?" Big difference. Bad people are capable of inexplicable nobility and good people can be meaner than skunks. Man is capable of larceny, rape, incest, murder, and all sorts of dark deeds that would horrify your average coyote, and that's a fact, so don't pretend that the Golden Rule is who we are. Mr. Larry was out to slit my throat, and I had to stop him by whatever means. *Simple as that.* Why waste time on moral indignation?

Sugar had loaded an app onto my cell phone so I could keep track of the blue ball that represented the Bogus Boy's scrotum, and it was sticking close to downtown St. Paul and spending plenty of time in and around the Acme Building. So it was time for me to decamp from the Shropshire Arms nearby and head across the river to Minneapolis. Sugar begged me to move in with her, but I am not a good roommate. I like to be able to put a Mose Allison record on the turntable and not be asked, "Who is he and why does he sing that way? Why the big vinyl disc? Why not a CD?" I also need to be able to go out the door and not be asked where I am going. Sometimes I don't know, myself. When I got a check for $158,000 on July 1, I made my move and called a real-estate agent. ("Darling," Naomi wrote, "Elongate is now sold in China, and it is such a sensation, there being no laws against worm medicinals there, and so I've opened a production plant in Chang-dao, and may be able to close down Mr. Ishimoto's operation in the near future. The Chinese plant has unlimited capacity, the sky's the limit.

We can now open sales offices in Beijing, New Delhi, Tokyo, Singapore, and Seoul. I'm in Paris, btw. I bought the sweetest little apartment near the Trocadero Gardens with a view of the Eiffel Tower through the French doors of my bedroom, and from my breakfast room, the Cathedral of Notre Dame. I do my exercises on parquet floors and out onto the balcony and down the grand staircase into the courtyard and around the fountain and out the gate and along the Seine, which is a stone's throw from my door. What a city!

"But I'm hoping to get home when the new book is done. Did I tell you about the new book? No? Well, all in good time.")

Though I walked through the valley of the shadow of death, the cash flow was strong, and my love life was picking up speed. One more reason to leave the dank and dismal Shropshire Arms and my eagle-eyed land-lady, Doris, taking note of my movements large and small, the contents of waste-baskets, the extent of my puzzling ("Can't do the Saturday crossword anymore, huh? My 12-year-old nephew does it in less than a half-hour."). The real estate agent was a dazzling beauty from Beige, Walz & Flors named Peyton Peterson, milky skin, golden hair, teeth aglow — I had to put on dark glasses to dim her luster.

"Location is everything, Guy," she said, putting her pale lilac-nailed hand on my shoulder, "and figures show that the hottest properties are close to water. I'm going to show you Pillsbury Mill condominiums overlooking St. Anthony Falls and downtown Minneapolis." Peyton could see I was moving up in the world, and she encouraged me to take a *big* leap and not inch my way up the slope. "Luxury properties hold their value better. Everyone knows that. You want to stay out of the midrange. It's taken some big hits." She took my elbow in her hand and fondled it. "I'm only guessing at what your financials are like, but I think you should aim for the $1.5 to $2.5 million range." This was heady stuff for a guy with a thousand-dollar-a-month studio apartment, and when a tall blonde says it and her hand is roaming up your back and coming to rest on the back of your neck, it sounds very reasonable.

It was July and the temperature hit 102 one day. Where, six months before, we'd been looking at an icy grave, now we were on the verge of combustion. Minnesota, the Theater of Seasons, and whether it's tragedy or comedy, we're never sure. The Shropshire Arms sat baking in the sun, and my little window air-conditioner was weeping softly to itself. I sat perspiring in my skivvies and felt like Willy Loman, and Peyton made me feel like I might become Henry IV. I made an appointment for Tuesday at noon.

My waistline was down to 30, lean as when I was twenty-one, and oddly, my hormones were kicking in big time thanks to a brisk thirty-minute walk every day and all those crunches and push-ups and squats, and women were all over me. They couldn't keep their hands off me. I was used to flirting with women and getting a sisterly pat on the shoulder and "Thanks but no thanks, Pops." My last pretapeworm romantic escapade was through Mercy Dating-dot-com, a walk around the block with a sixty-five-year-old twice-divorced woman looking for a short-term relationship while the swelling went down from her plastic surgery. But now I was hot merch. In the Brew Ha Ha, young women, art students, twenty-one, twenty-two years old, would walk right up and grab my shirt and say how much they loved the nubbliness of the material, the color, the drape, the indescribable *feel* of it, and all the time their fingers were walking over my pecs, making my epidermis tingle and my heart go boom. A slight girl with flaming red hair approached and asked where did you get those cargo pants and she grabbed a handful of inner leg and said, "I really love this" — that never happened to me pretapeworm.

It's a man's daydream to be accosted and jostled and fingered and poked by beautiful women. I sat working the *Times* crossword, and a young beauty brushed her breasts against my earlobe and whispered, "I don't mean to interrupt but I think that twenty-one across, where you wrote INTOTHE-FORESTQUICKLY — actually that should be INTELLIGENCEQUOTIENT." And she put her finger on it — "Right there, twenty-one across" — which also brought her pelvic mound up tight to my right shoulder. Caramba! Lord, have mercy!

"I see you here in the coffee shop a lot," she said.

"I see you just as much," I said.

"Are you a writer?"

I shook my head. "Wouldn't even consider it. Writers are snoops and sneaks and betrayers of friends and family. No, I'm a security consultant. I protect people. Do you need protection?"

She gave me a look. "I think I can handle that," she said. "But here's my number if you want to talk some more."

The excitement of that dewy-eyed, fresh-faced physical presence — the unforgettableness of her — pretty much destroyed the rest of my day. She wrote her phone number down on a slip of paper, and I stared at it and asked myself, *Does a twenty-two-year-old really need to have an aging PI in her life, and do I want to be a father figure to a naked person?* The correct answers are *no* and *no.* I tried to argue myself out of the correct answers (*Life is meant to be enjoyed, and what harm can come of a little romantic fling? Correct answer: A whole lot.*) without success.

But Sugar was crazy about me. Birch Bergquist, too, I was pretty sure. Sharon at the Brew Ha Ha hit on me. Twice. Told me she was "dying of loneliness." Asked what I was "up to tonight" and did I want to "hang out" at her apartment? She thought we had "a lot in common" — this from a woman of twenty-seven to a man in what I think of as my extremely late fifties. I looked at her raven tresses falling onto her bare shoulders like dark chocolate on vanilla, and suddenly I had a craving for sweets. I told her I was busy tonight but to keep me in mind. "Oh, I've got you in mind," she murmured, and she grabbed my butt and squeezed. Took the whole right cheek in her hand like she was checking out a melon and said, "I've got plans for you, sweetie."

What a pleasure. A mangy mutt becomes a show dog and — *bow wow wow* — what a difference a little glamour makes! My world was golden. A woman named Nell sought my professional help. She taught eleventh-grade English — though, looking at her, it was hard to see how boys in her class could stay focused on Shakespeare — and she'd created a computer program that could read and grade student term papers on *Huckleberry Finn, Macbeth, Beloved, The Scarlet Letter, Death of a Salesman,* and *The Great Gatsby,* and write cogent comments in the margins, a fabulous time saver, and she was looking for a way to market it.

"You came to the wrong guy," I said. "I've got no head for business."

"What do you have a head for?" she said in a seductive tone. She put her small, pale hand on my shoulder.

"Eyes to behold you, ears to hear you, a tongue to speak."

She recognized the quote from something, I forget what, and she asked me what I wanted to say.

I thought about that for a moment. "I want to be with you and make you happy in a way you've never been happy before," I said.

She said, "I told my husband I was going canoeing."

"With him?"

She shook her head. "He doesn't do outdoor things. He's allergic to bug bites. One little mosquito bite, and he swells up like a puff pastry."

I nodded.

"So let's go canoeing," she murmured.

I tried to say no, but what came out was "Of course."

Love was in the air, and the sweet scent of apples and old leather, horses, smoke, dry leaves. The waves softly lapping on the shore of Lake Como, as she paddled the rental canoe into a secluded inlet in the shade of a weeping willow, my head in her lap, feeling her thighs twist as she pushed the canoe along. She leaned down and kissed me on the lips and inserted her tongue. She squeezed my arm and said I was exactly her type, whatever that means. I told her that her grading software would be a godsend to teachers and free them from the grind of paperwork so they could look at the bigger picture, my own eyes at the moment focused upward on her low-cut black blouse that gave new meaning to the words *va va va voom.* Her delicate fingers unbuttoned the top three buttons of my shirt and clearly we were headed for a collision in one bed or another. But which one? Her husband was at home, my apartment was a horror show. So I called up the Hotel Bel Rive and got onto a complicated touch-tone menu — pressed one for Reservations and then four for Today's Reservations and three for No, I Am Not a Member of the Concierge Club. I was on hold for a minute, listening to a woman sing about a romantic weekend for two with complimentary champagne and in-room massage and floral bouquet, and then a live woman came on and asked if I would mind being put on hold for a minute, so I went back to the singer and the champagne weekend. A recorded voice thanked me for my patience and said someone would be with me shortly. It was a little aggravating, knowing that my inability to order up a room must be raising questions in the mind of the potential lover sitting patiently in the bow of the canoe, waving away the gnats and horseflies, so when finally the live woman came on and said, "Yes, we have a room with king-size bed for $149.50. May I have your credit card number?" I rose to my feet to pull out my billfold and, of course, capsized the canoe, and not in a grand or heroic way — I simply toppled over like a stooge in a movie — and Nell screamed and fell into the water too, which was about four feet deep there. We stood up, soaking wet, and looked at each other. She wasn't laughing. I had dropped my billfold in the lake and also her cell phone. We felt around in the mucky bottom with our feet and didn't locate them. This took twenty minutes or so. She asked me if I had ever been canoeing before. Her tone of voice stung me to the quick. And then she looked at her watch and announced that she had to be home in fifteen minutes, which clearly was a lie. Another insult. So that was that. Farewell, Nell.

Jimmy the bartender always asks me how my love life is, and I told him about Nell and Sugar and Sharon and all the twentyish ladies who took a shine to me, and he says, "See? I told you a dozen times. Get rid of the grunge look and rejoin the human race." He was putting crushed ice in the martini shaker, and I told him not to put so much in, which he ignored. "You thought it was hip to look like a homeless person, and that may be true when you're young, but past thirty-five it doesn't work anymore, and that's why you used to come in here all sad and rejected and feeling morbid and morose and needing a jolt of gin to pull you out of the nosedive, but would you listen to me? No." He poured in too much vermouth, as he always does, but I said nothing. "Now you've lost forty pounds and your abs are no longer like a big pillow, and you got your teeth cleaned and found a good cologne instead of the sheep disinfectant you used to use, and no wonder the women are sniffing around you."

And then a woman walked up as I drank the martini and whispered that I made her think bad thoughts. Her name was Kendra. She looked to be in her late sixties but in fact she was thirty-seven — she'd taught eighth-grade English for ten years, and it had aged her. "I live not far from here," she said. "Forgive me for being direct, but — do you want to do stuff?" she said.

"Do stuff?"

"Do stuff with me." And she clicked her tongue. Jimmy stood rearranging bottles on the back bar, listening intently.

I told her I had to get home to the wife and kiddos.

She sneered. "You ain't married, mister. I know Married, and you're not in that particular league."

"How do you know that?"

"You look all cheery and shiny, that's how. You look like nobody's yelled at you in months."

"Four or five guys are out to shoot me in the head, but never mind that. Small detail." I put down a ten for the drink and she and I strolled over to her apartment in the Angus Hotel on Selby Avenue. Books were strewn everywhere, and a brown shag carpet looked like buffalo had slept on it. The smell of burnt incense. A public radio station was in the throes of Pledge Week, and a weepy woman was on the air, crying, "Please, please call the eight hundred number now — if I don't hear from ten of you right now, I am going to have my cat put to sleep! I'm not kidding. I don't want my Mittens to live in a world where people don't care about quality broadcasting!" And she broke down, sobbing, and Kendra turned the radio off and started unbuttoning her blouse as she asked me if I had read much Flannery O'Connor.

"I don't go for Southern literature," I said. "It makes me perspire and it makes me itch."

"Unsnap my bra," she whispered. "What about Faulkner? I love *Absalom, Absalom*." The bra fell to the floor. Her nipples were large and funguslike. I looked away.

"Are you into restraint?" she said.

"Self-restraint?"

She made a face. "Have you ever tied a woman's wrists and ankles to a bed? It's only an idea. We don't have to do it. But if you would — and if you would sprinkle kitty litter on me, I get all hot and tingly."

"I don't think this is going to work out," I said. I got to the door, though she clung to my lapels and was swinging her breasts from side to side, trying to arouse interest. "Touch my perfect body with your mind," she said.

"I have to tell you something. I'm gay," I said. And I sang a little bit of "Somewhere over the Rainbow" in a high trembly voice, and she kissed me good-bye. "I hope you find someone to love," she said. "And call me if you decide you want to experiment."

The Pillsbury Mill condo that Peyton showed me was a two-bedroom on the sixth floor, with thirteen-foot ceilings and enormous windows overlooking the Mississippi waters churning below, the dam and locks, the Stone Arch bridge, the towers of downtown, and Nicollet Island — she gave me a full tour of the joint, and I couldn't remember a thing except how my heart leaped up when she asked me if I would be living there alone. "I hope not!" I cried. *Got any ideas?* I thought. "I'm sort of in between relationships right now," I explained. "Been thinking maybe it's time to settle down," I offered. A few minutes later I had forked over a down payment of $175,138 and signed the mortgage and shaken her hand on the deal.

"Any advice on decoration?" I asked.

"If it were me, I'd do minimalist."

"I was hoping you'd say that! It'll be minimalist all the way. I can minimize with the best of them!"

I was sort of distracted by Peyton, and not until I moved into 619 did I notice there were no cupboards, no stove or washer or dryer, and no wood flooring in the bedroom, just rough plywood with big splinters. Ah well. A person can always carpet a bedroom. I looked around my little domain and thought, *Here is where I will be finally happy again. Here is where I will bring her, whoever she may be, and here she and I will make a good life together.* I missed having a woman in my life. The pantyhose on the shower rod, the doodads around the bathroom sink. The cat hair. The wet towels on the bathroom floor. The monthly emotional meltdown and the weeping and accusations. The hour-long phone conversations with the girlfriend in

California while the two of them paint their toenails. The handwriting with the little heart shape dotting the I on the note you find in the morning on the bedside table, *darling i am so sorry i called you a shithead last night. i want you to know i love you & there is nobody like you. xxxxxoxoxox.* The stuffed animals in the bed. The anger toward the mother. The vast arsenal of beauty products that takes over the entire bathroom. I miss all of that.

I moved out of the Shropshire Arms on August 1, me and a U-Haul trailer, assisted by a pimply faced kid named Kevin. And my landlady, Doris, hands on hips, telling me what a big mistake I was making, that real-estate values were in the toilet, and that I was about to lose my shirt, and where'd I come by all that money anyway, was I selling drugs or what? If so, did I expect her to take me back after I was indicted and the condo gone back to the bank? Well, think again.

I had saved her life one summer night when I whacked her on the back and dislodged an ice cube from her epiglottis as she was choking to death on her rum and Coke, and she never forgave me for the favor. "No good deed goes unpunished," as they say. She was furious at her late husband Sidney, who ran off with a twenty-five-year-old named Chrysalis the day Doris had four wisdom teeth pulled and was heading home from the dentist zonked on Vicodin and a teenager stole her purse with her car keys in it so she had to walk twenty-seven blocks home and got there to find her husband's note saying, "I have found a love so rare that I cannot walk away from it. Chrysalis completes me as I've never been completed before. I wish you all the best." And also the toilet had overflowed. From this afternoon of horror she became a gimlet-eyed harpy, and I was the one available for harping on. Sidney was not, having died, drunk and desolate, when Chrysalis left him for a personal trainer. (Doris scattered his ashes in a hazardous waste site.) Doris's apartment was just inside the front door and whenever I came home late I could hear her listening to my tippy-toe footsteps, trying to discern if two other feet were tiptoeing alongside mine. She loathed me, which was her form of love, and when I told her I had put money down on a two-bedroom in a luxury high-rise overlooking the Mississippi, she was heartbroken. "You'll be living on the street before Christmas," she said. "Wait and see. A big cardboard carton on the steps of a church and a tangle of ratty blankets and a hand-lettered sign:

HOPELESS FOOL WHO NEVER LISTENED TO ANYBODY AND NOW LOOK AT HIM. HERE BUT FOR THE GRACE OF GOD, ETC. PLEASE HELP IF YOU CAN. HAVE A NICE DAY."

"Why do you always assume the worst about me?" I said.

"You really want to know?" she replied. "Are you not aware of what I've put up with for the past fifteen years?"

"Why don't you just say, 'Good luck, Guy, and I hope you're happy'? Why the insults and accusations?"

"How can you do something so stupid as this? Where are your brains? In your butt?"

I was getting hot under the collar. "Why is it so difficult for you to utter a simple declarative sentence? Why talk only in questions?"

"You want a declarative sentence? Is that what you really want?" she said, jabbing me with her index finger. "Or are you just trying to irritate me by acting like an irresponsible idiot?"

"Why does a simple request always turn into an exchange of insults? Why are you so bitter?"

"Am I supposed to care what you think? Why should I?"

"When are you going to get over Sidney and find a life, Doris? When?"

"What business is that of yours? What do you know about anything?"

And then I lowered the boom on her.

"May I have my damage deposit back, please?"

She took her sweet time, examining every nook and cranny of my apartment, counting scratch marks on the floor, before she shelled out the deposit, $75.75. I took the dough and gave it to an old wino stationed in front of Central Presbyterian. He took it, blinked, cleared his throat, and said, "Think you could see your way clear to making it an even hundred bucks?" So I shelled out an additional $25. A reward for chutzpah.

# 15
## ENTER MR. FREUD

I kept waiting for Mr. Larry to come around and settle my hash, and he didn't and didn't, and I know that game, the waiting game. You want your prey to go crazy wondering where you are and when you'll show up, and pretty soon you've taken control of their mind day and night. *Where's Larry? Is he standing just outside that door? Is he going to beat it down and come in roaring and bust me in the chops?* It's an old psychological game, Waiting for the Last Trump & the Judgment. The day I moved into Pillsbury Mill, he called, just so I'd know he knew where I was. "Nice apartment, pal, very classy," he said on the phone. "But when I told you to get out of town, I didn't mean Minneapolis — that's just a suburb. I meant, *way* out of town. And you gotta hand over the worms. My patience is running out. And when I hit you, it's gonna hurt. I'm gonna squash you like a

June bug. Boom. You're outta here. I got friends among the meathead element. Your punks, your shooters. They envy my lifestyle. So don't jerk me around, Noir, or else. Boom. I want the worms in forty-eight hours, or else my boys are gonna put you six feet under where the worms can have their way with you." I could hear him gnashing his teeth. He wanted me to know that he meant business.

I woke up one morning tangled in the sheets after a bad dream in which I was chased down a dark alley and had to hide in a Dumpster and I remembered suddenly a photo I'd seen a year or two before in *Radio & TV Times* of Mr. Larry arm in arm with Boyd Freud, co-anchor of Channel 5's *News About You,* the news show with the big cooking segment and tips on relationships and skin care. I looked it up online, and indeed, the two appeared to be thick as thieves. ("Anchorman Boyd Freud and longtime associate Larry B. [L.B.] Larry at benefit for homeless.") I happened to have met Mr. Freud at Sugar O'Toole's birthday party years before, and I called him up at the TV station. "Noir. Guy Noir. We met at Sugar's a long time ago, and we talked about arachnids."

He remembered. I chatted him up and we met for coffee that afternoon at a noisy joint in Prospect Park.

Boyd was the male Caucasian news anchor with big hair that Channel 5 paired with Nevaeh Evans, the beautiful minority woman co-anchor with sardonic eyes, and Steve, the dorky meteorologist, and Artie, the goofball sports guy who bounces up and down in his chair like he's wetting his pants. Mr. Freud sat slumped in a back booth, dark glasses, glum, chewing a cracker, as I walked in. He didn't look at all like the hearty news guy on TV. I asked him why the long puss, and he told me his approval numbers were way down and Nevaeh's were up, and he lived in dread of getting canned and having to go to a smaller market like Sioux Falls or Grand Forks. He wrung his hands at the thought. A marketing wizard at Channel Five had dreamed up a promotion, whereby Boyd would marry Nevaeh on the air, the culmination of a three-month courtship. She was agreeable but on one condition: she'd become the head anchor and do hard news, and he'd do human interest stories, interview small children, cover fairs and carnivals, and do a daily feature called "Animal Friends" in which he'd talk about an iguana or shrew or possum or garter snake, while holding the critter in his hands. Also, she wanted a bonus of a half-million dollars.

Boyd was sick at the thought; he was not fond of animals. "I am in a living hell. I've gained thirty-seven pounds in the past two months. I'm looking blobby on the screen."

"We can help each other," I said. "I can give you a guaranteed weight-loss pill, and I can give you some leverage with Nevaeh. You can give me Larry B. Larry, who is trying to horn in on a business deal."

"Larry, that rat! He's supposed to be my agent, and he's done nothing for me! Nada! Zilch! Count me in." We shook hands on it. He told me that Mr. Larry had a truckload of gambling debts and money was his one and only motive — so he could be negotiated with.

Same afternoon. Lieutenant McCafferty called up and said, "I hear you're hanging out with the Bogus Brothers."

I told him I was trying to avoid the Bogus Brothers on account of they were attempting to take my scalp.

"I'm just saying I'd watch who I keep company with if I were you."

I told him again that I didn't want to get anywhere near the Bogus Brothers.

"I'm just saying that if I see you with them, I'm going to have to draw my own conclusions, Noir."

McCafferty is not the brightest bulb in the field of law enforcement. He was once trying to track down a jazz bassist who had swiped a ukulele, and he collared a guy in the park — he said, "You're a jazzer. You're wearing dark glasses after dark."

"I'm visually impaired," the guy yelled. "Okay? See the white cane?" He whacked it on the sidewalk, and a German shepherd woke up and stood by his side. "See the dog? You blind or something?"

"Sorry. Didn't notice."

"Use your eyes, for crying out loud. Jeez."

Anyway, that's McCafferty.

I did some scouting around on Nevaeh and found an old boyfriend named Mutt Mullins who she picked up back when she was a telemarketer and called to ask if he'd like to save 25 percent on his texting charges and he said he never texted and she said, "How can that be?" and he said it took too long pecking one-fingered at the tiny keyboard on his phone screen and she said, "Use both thumbs," and she offered to show him how and that's how they got together. He was a mutt, and she was attracted to mutts. She

187

moved into his apartment and dumped two Dumpsters full of his debris and refinished his floors and hung designer shades and cleaned out his closet and dressed him in classy clothes. He was the one who told her she should be in TV and introduced her to his brother Mike, a TV director, who hired her, and she promptly dumped Mutt for a sports anchor who was handsomer and happier, and Mutt was still bitter about that. He was a security man at a self-storage complex called Closet Warehouse, an octopuslike monstrosity of one-story cinderblock wings of windowless storage units that people rented to keep their junk in, out on Interstate 35W, across Maplelawn Boulevard from Pepe's Pants Warehouse, Chris Wilmot's Home of Hope Tabernacle, and Dave's Drive-Through Desserts, which was featuring a Six-Scoop Hot Fudge Sundae. "We were in journalism school together, and she was good-looking and minority, so she got on a career track, and I'm white and got a mug like a shovel, and here I am, an attendant at a parking lot for flotsam and jetsam. That's how the cookie crumbles, it's all about looks."

He was glad to tell me that in her college days she'd smoked dope and done pills, and once she posed nude for a men's magazine called *Nooner.*

"Really," I said. "That'd be something of interest."

He offered to sell me a copy for fifty dollars.

The magazine was in his own storage unit, a twelve-by-twelve bin with a single folding chair, a hand-sanitizer dispenser, a lightbulb hanging on a cord over stacks of *Playboy, Penthouse, Maxim, Gape, Ogle,* and *I-Ball* magazines, and file cabinets with clippings of photos filed by breast types — Titties, Gumdrops, Casabas, Chi-Chis, Bobblers, Missiles, Maracas, and O Mammy. "Nevaeh was a Gumdrop," he informed me, handing me the mag. It was her, and she was naked all right. She was lolling in a pink 1957 Pontiac parked under pine trees, and her breasts, pert and perky, nested quite prettily against her rib cage. "Lissome, alluring Nevaeh Evans takes a break from her journalism studies at St. Cloud State to bathe her beauty in solar rays," etc., etc.

Mr. Mullins's breath was faintly fermented. Watching over storage units evidently left plenty of time for relaxation. "I applied for a janitor job at Channel Five and called her to see if she'd put in a good word for me, and she acted like she'd never heard my name before. We were in a *relation-*

189

*ship,* man. We slept in a bed together. I helped her write her papers. Then when I was no longer of use, she dumped me like an old newspaper."

I felt queasy about the whole deal. The exposure of a news anchor's youthful indiscretion is nothing to be proud of. I never was a shining star in the Ethics Department, but I didn't want to be involved in destroying a young woman's career. Her boss was the bullet-headed right-wing tycoon and half-wit loudmouth Stanley Mutter — and the thought of him eyeballing this lovely, vulnerable, unclothed person was repellent to me. I opened the magazine to page fifty-two, and it was all so clear, her innocence, her good-heartedness, her need — some man had sweet-talked her into posing, lying naked on her side across the hood of the car, the hood ornament between her ankles, and he'd paid her a hundred dollars, which seemed like easy money to her, not knowing that it could come back years later and blow up in her face and ruin her career.

*On the other hand,* maybe this was the sort of scandal that PR people yearn for — a big boomer of a story that lands smack dab on page one:

## NUDE PIX OF NEWS ANCHOR EXPOSED; "NEVAEH, HOW COULD YOU?" CRY FANS; CHANNEL 5 ORDERS 2-DAY SUSPENSION

And two days later, the exposée weeps ("I was young! I was foolish!") and begs for forgiveness ("My viewers are the most important people in my life") and announces she's going into treatment ("I am a serial exhibitionist and this is my opportunity to confront my demons"). She returns ten days later, does a guest shot on talk radio, and tells about her obsessive need for male approval that led her to do that shameful thing, and is forgiven, and becomes *twice as popular as ever before.*

Sending the issue of *Nooner* to Gene Willikers might be the biggest favor anyone ever did for Nevaeh.

*On the other hand* — what if it wasn't?

I turned once again to page fifty-two in hopes of getting some guidance from the young, lissome beauty reclining on the Pontiac, her lovely head against the windshield, arms flung to either side, long legs splayed, a faint patina of goose bumps on her dark skin — she looked like someone who could easily lure sailors to their deaths. Would this maiden choose broad dissemination of her image, or would she prefer to draw a curtain of privacy?

I parked in front of the Channel 5 building, pondering this issue, and spotted the Eyewitness News van (*News 4 U@ 6 & 10*) with the satellite dish on top, and there on the sidewalk stood Nevaeh herself, microphone in hand, as the cameraman waited and a poofy-haired man brushed powder on her beautiful countenance and got out a mascara pencil. "Close your eyes," he said, and so she didn't see me when I walked up. On the grass behind her, standing ramrod straight at attention, was the Anoka High School Marching Band in maroon and gray uniforms, eighty strong, clarinets in front, six silver tubas in back, the plump, fish-faced director standing to the side, the drum major in white poised to give the downbeat. I put the magazine in her hand. "Someone is trying to blackmail you, and it isn't me," I said. "By the way, you have terrific tits." And I gave a big thumbs-up to the drum major, who took me for a TV producer, and the drums hit four big beats and a long roll and blazed out with "The Minnesota Rouser." But I was already aroused. If Nevaeh had made a pass at me, I would've scooped her up right there and then and headed for the airport. She looked like she was about to. She glanced at the porn and looked up at me and touched her bosom and whispered, "Thank you." But before she could say more, I felt severe gastric disturbances and moved at a quick trot toward the street, and a whisper of gas escaped from me, and I got in the car and peeled out. I felt heat in the gluteal cleft. I opened the windows and let go of it, a long trombone blast, a cloud of evil shooting out, rattling the aperture, and I decided then and there to put the worms to death and resume normal life.

# 16
## SCARLETT

Naomi had warned me that the process of ridding oneself of tapeworms is not pleasant. She had killed hers off in Paris, and there was, she said, a lot of writhing around and some bloating and blasting and other sorts of abdominal turmoil while she sat on the porcelain throne and then gradually, grudgingly, they came out, still twitching, great long lengths of them, slimy, blue-green, swimming around in the toilet bowl, and thank goodness Johnny was there to clean up the mess. (She didn't say who Johnny was, and that's good because I didn't want to know.)

I had set up camp in my new apartment and steeled myself to the task ahead and took my position on the throne, with bicarbonate of soda at hand and also a ballpeen hammer in case the creatures needed pacification, and I held the yellow pill in my hand and was about to swallow it when the phone rang, and like a fool I answered. It was Naomi, calling from New York.

"Hi. How are you doing?" she said. No "Darling I miss you" or "I count the hours until I see you" — just the "Hi. How are you doing?" A sign that something was amiss. She was sitting in a café on West 67th Street, waiting to go into ABC-TV and tape an interview with Phil Ragbin, the aging co-host of the *Chloris & Phil* show, to promote her brand-new book — "New book??" said I. "Why? How?"

"I have a brilliant writer named Billy Williams. I'm way too busy promoting books to keep writing them, and he *loves* to sit in a dim cubicle all day and flesh out my ideas, so what the hey. The book is called *The Blessing of Less,* and it basically says that weight loss is an act of religious devotion, and it's forty-four pages long, and my publicist says it's shooting straight to number one on the *Times* best-seller list. Anyway — I called because I need you to take care of something. Remember Larry B. Larry?"

"He's been threatening me with bodily harm for the past month. Yeah. I'm well aware of the guy."

"Well, Mr. Larry has gone and sold an option on Elongate to Pfizer. Pfizer, the pharmaceuticals giant. They gave him a half million to deliver the DNA of our tapeworms. And Pfizer has a mole in the Food and Drug Administration named Cliff Kress, who is about to usher their version of Elongate through the licensing process. We're in an ambush by giants, Guy. I've got my lawyer Birch on the case, but I need you to scout the opposition. This Kress is based in Minneapolis, a mild-mannered bow-tie sort of guy who adores French pastry and Marcel Proust and hopes to retire to an apartment in Provence in a few months, and he's in Pfizer's pocket. I'd like you to drop some cash in his small white palm and see if he might cut us some slack. We can afford the dough."

Elongate had done six million in sales in one week, she told me. The big sales bulge was among women forty-eight to sixty-four, the gals with the harem pants and the voluminous shirts, and after that, men eighteen to thirty-five, the nerds who sit at computers day and night and snack on Cheez-Its and apple fritters and develop a ring of blubber over their belt. And then there are the grossly obese who live in darkened apartments with no mirrors, in buildings with freight elevators, who feed on ginormous pepperoni pizzas, two at a sitting, and earn their living as telemarketers. Elongate had made a big splash in the fattycake world. Naomi told me this in a dispassionate way, as if she were telling about something she'd read in the paper. She was no longer het up about tapeworms. She had moved off in pursuit of Lessness.

It dawned on me then that the big checks might stop coming. A gift horse that falls into your lap can just as easily fall out of your lap. And my lap was not as large as it had been.

"Are you coming back to Minnesota?" I asked, and as the words came out of my mouth, I knew the answer. When you are conquering the world, why would you turn around and come home?

"Oh darling, I miss the Mississippi, but a girl has to cut hay while the sun shines, and I don't know anybody back there anymore except you and some lady professors, and they all hate me because I got too successful. If you're a feminist academic, you're supposed to be unappreciated and bitter, and here I am with a Paris apartment and I just bought the most darling little cottage in Southampton. It *feels* little but it's eight thousand square feet, and I would love to show it to *you,* darling, but if I had lunch with those ladies, they'd sit and loathe me unless I made up a story about having

197

pancreatic cancer, and that would give them such pleasure, they'd almost forgive me for being rich and beautiful."

She sighed, and I waited for her to suggest a specific time when she might show me the cottage in Southampton, but she swept on. "*The Blessing of Less* is going to be huge, darling. It's gathering slowly, like a tidal wave, and it's going to start a revolution in this country. *Less* is the new *More*. It's not only about weight loss, it's about the power of diminishment. Concentration. The beauty of the minimal. Politics, the arts, religion — it is relevant across the board. Walmart ordered a hundred thousand copies. Oprah is making it her Book Club selection. The Dalai Lama is sending it to everyone on his Christmas card list."

"How long will you be in New York?" I said.

"Only two days, then I'm off to Mexico with Rush Limbaugh and that big fatso governor of New Jersey, Mr. Chris Misty. Rush is on the pill. He lost forty pounds in the first month, and it's making him sensitive and wistful, and he wants to quit his attack-dog radio show and become a children's author. He's working on a book called *Lillian the Llama,* and we're going to his llama ranch in Michoacán and just lie in a steam bath and cleanse."

She was so happy I didn't have the heart to tell her about all the women who were after me. Even as she talked about Lessness, Sharon was texting me: *The smell of espresso makes me horny since you were in here yesterday. I just want to rip your clothes off. Just saying. Oh, by the way, good morning.*

I checked my phone, and the blue ball was in Minneapolis, moving slowly west on Wayzata Boulevard, so I dropped in at the Brew Ha Ha to tell Sharon I'd moved, in case (hint hint) she wanted to come over and check out the bedspreads. The place was jammed with art students, and she was in excellent form, snarffling a pitcher of milk to a fine froth, and asking an old guy if he wanted any sprinkles, hinkles, or dinkles on his latte — he shook his head — and I strolled over. She whispered behind her hand: "What's going on with you? I heard you moved to a fancy-schmancy place on the river."

"Who told you that?"

"A guy named Mr. Larry. He was in here looking for you."

"Why would he look here if he knew I was over there?"

And the old guy turned and said that if

this was the same Larry B. Larry as the one he knew, then I'd be well advised to hightail it to Chicago and keep going. He took his latte, and Sharon leaned over and said, "You and I going to spend some time together?"

"Let's do that. We've known each other a long time. It's time we should get to know each other."

She reached down under the counter and hauled out a box the size of a hatbox, wrapped in brown paper and tied up in string. "Mr. Larry left this for you," she said.

I lifted it. It was very light. Nothing ticked or hissed inside. I shook it, and nothing was loose. *Anthrax,* I thought. *A batch of botulism.* But of course the guy wouldn't want to kill me quite yet, not until I handed over the queens.

"He didn't head upstairs, by any chance, did he?"

She shook her head. "Left here and got into a black Lincoln Town Car and was on his cell phone the whole time. So how are you?"

I wanted to tell her that I had become a sex symbol, but it isn't the sort of thing you should have to explain to people.

I shook the box again and thumped it, and then I stripped off the paper and string and slowly opened the top flaps and looked in, and there, glued to the bottom, was the cigar box from my desk. The box I'd stored the worms in. Empty.

Out the door I ran and buzzed the elevator and rode up to the twelfth floor and around the corner, and my office door was ajar. Inside, a maelstrom of paper. Mounds of it. Files strewn hither and yon, and the queen worms gone without a trace.

I called Mr. Ishimoto. He was not perturbed.

"The good queens I have shipped to China," he said. "The ones I gave you are bad queens. Very bad, Mistah Cholly." I heard an insidious chuckle. "Whoever takes the eggs of those queens will get a big surprise. No babies. No sex." He burst into high-pitched giggles.

I came back to the Brew Ha Ha and took my espresso to an empty table next to the window looking out at the park where the bums reclined on the benches around the granite fountain. The bum life had appealed to me at one time, the thought of napping in parks and arranging one's social life around the soup kitchen at the Dorothy Day Center and planning the fall migration to warmer climes. There is intelligent life among the unemployed. You learn about that if you hoof it around town and meet people rather than ride around locked up in a car — there are learned philosophers in Palmer's and the 400 Bar near Seven Corners, and if you appreciate the art of the storyteller, you will find better practitioners in bars and on city buses than in any creative writing program. Storytelling and panhandling are allied crafts: a writer in no need of ready cash is only going through the motions, like a hockey player without a puck or a horseman on a sawhorse. I had lost the precious tapeworm queens only to discover that they were worse than worthless, they were poison.

And should I now call Mr. Larry and warn him? Or let him find out that his pencil will soon have no more lead?

A slim young thing walked over to me, wearing one of those light summer dresses that you just know women who wear them know what they do to men. I mean, ventilation is not all that's going on here. She had wild kinky black hair and heavy eyebrows and a sullen mouth that I wanted to kiss. "Mind if I sit down?" she said. The bodice of her dress was cut in an interesting way — it was simply two long vertical straps that revealed the sides and undersides of her breasts. Which were perfection, the Monet

*Water Lilies* of breasts.

She sat down opposite me and flashed a flicker of a smile. "You Noir? Guy Noir?"

"If you want me to be someone else, just say."

"I'm here to meet a friend."

"You just did. Me. Where have you been all my life, gorgeous?"

"Well, for the first half of your life, I wasn't born yet."

Her voice was slightly hoarse. A wisp of smoke twisted out of her mouth as she said my name, and then I saw the cigarette. She tapped the ash into her palm and brushed back a mass of black curls. "My name is Scarlett. Scarlett Anderson. I like noirish stuff. Especially the movies. The ones where the hero is seriously screwed up and the romantic lead is a bad woman and people tend to have dark secrets, especially the cops." She stubbed the smoke out on the floor. "By the way," she said, "I'm packing a heater. A Glock. Just so you know. I do it for the thrill. That scare you? Woman with a roscoe?" She grinned. "Or maybe it excites you."

I was looking her in the eye, trying not to stare at her breasts, and then I simply had to look. They were proud things, well defined, sculpted, the nipples erect under the cloth. The gun, by the looks of things, was in her tote bag. It certainly wasn't under her dress.

"You come here often, Mr. Noir? You look very comfortable."

"I do. I like the context. Young people and their creative aspirations."

She smiled. "Do you have creative aspirations?"

"None, whatsoever. I'm strictly a voyeur."

"I can see that, the way you're looking me over." She pulled a cigarette out of somewhere, I didn't see where, I was looking elsewhere. "I like to be looked at. And there's a lot more of me to look at than what you're seeing right now. If you were a painter, I'd offer to model for you."

"If you were my model, I'd for sure try to be a painter."

"Whatever you did would be just wonderful, I'm sure. So long as it came from pure feeling." The way she said "pure feeling" made my skin follicles take a deep breath.

She lit the cigarette. Minnesota has been a No Smoking state for so long, people around us were staring at her as if she had stepped out of a history book. She blew a great cloud of smoke into the air, and they shuddered and crouched down to avoid it as it drifted across the room, as if it were radioactive. They were too young to remember when people used to do this.

"I've always been drawn to older men with aspirations," she whispered. "I'm twenty-three years old, and so I have a lot of older men to choose from. I like to *experience* men who are experienced. Men who bear the burden of age and disappointment and loss but their hearts still can leap. And frankly, I like the looks of you. Some men are put off by a woman who is frank about what she wants. Well, Mr. Noir" — she put her hand on mine — "when I see what I want, I take it, and there's not much anybody can do about it." She leaned forward and slid her chair around toward mine. I could feel my blood pressure rising. And something else. "I think I can make your heart leap, Mr. Noir. I am fairly certain of that."

Suddenly I had a picture in my mind of her naked, standing in an open window, sunlight around her like an aura, the pale skin of her long legs, her radiant thighs, her womanhood, and my heart did sort of leap. Not as high as once it did long ago when Beatrice Olsen wrapped her legs around me, but high enough. And it could learn to leap higher.

"By the way, I'm from Pfizer," she said,

putting a hand on my leg. "You know. The drug company. I've been talking to a Mr. Ishimoto, who I believe you know. The name ring a bell?"

"Ding."

"And what about Naomi Fallopian?"

"Ding. Ding. Ding."

She smiled. "Good. Then you know what brings me here." She had the advantage of surprise, and also she had her hand on my leg. "America is a great country, Mr. Noir, and every so often some enterprising entrepreneur gets lucky with an invention such as your little pill, Elongate, and they have visions of wealth and success, and they try to go it alone, and the outcome is not good. No, it is not. They're like a rowboat in a busy harbor where big ships are steaming to and fro, and they wind up getting smashed and sinking to the bottom and — guess what? — nobody even knows they existed. I happen to know exactly how much you've been paid by Miss Fallopian." She pulled out a paper and pencil from her tote bag — I glanced down and saw the butt of the Glock wrapped in a red silk hanky — and wrote down a six-figure sum that looked pretty accurate to me.

"We can do better than that, Mr. Noir. A lot better." And the hand on my leg slid upward. "Pfizer is a giant cash machine. The big money in America used to be in gold or oil or manufacturing cars, but now it's in feel-good pharmaceuticals. Half of all Americans are on medications now, and in ten years that number will be up to three-quarters. We're developing drugs to combat discouragement, boredom, ennui, revulsion, fear of death, all the negative emotions once considered inevitable in life, and these drugs can keep a person's chemistry beautifully balanced at a high peak of lightheartedness. In ten years, nobody in America will experience loneliness at all. It will disappear, like smallpox. Pfizer has been working on a weight-loss drug for years, and we think that your drug can give us a new angle. It's rather crude. Side effects include dizziness, heightened libido, loss of inhibitions, and flatulence. You give that pill to a thousand people, and you'll have about 128 of them running around naked, throwing themselves at strangers, and farting up a storm. Whatever Pfizer develops will be nothing so primitive as tapeworms, but the chemistry is interesting. And that's why we need your queens. There's some DNA there that we can't retrieve through reverse engineering."

Her hand was now up around my pants pocket. "Did you know that Pfizer owns the name Elongate? We trademarked it for the drug that came to be called Viagra instead. So we have grounds for an enormous messy lawsuit that I'm afraid would be personally disastrous for you, sweetheart. Pfizer uses attorneys as casually as you and I use Q-tips. I could make a phone call this afternoon, and tomorrow morning you'd have a man at your door with a two-pound subpoena, and you'd be in for four years of misery that would leave you limp as a used tea bag and a couple million in debt. Miss Fallopian can gallivant around Paris, heedless of American law, but here you are, easy prey. Why go down that chute and land in the sewer? And that doesn't include the misery of having the feds on your case. There are laws about drugs, you know. A drug like yours needs to be brought into the market very, very carefully, and that means seducing the FDA."

I pulled back. Her hand had reached a critical spot.

"It isn't a medication," I said weakly. "It's an entirely natural substance, like butter or cheese."

"And what does the F in FDA stand for? Flatulence?"

"It's not a food either. It's an antifood."

"Then it's a med."

I wasn't sure what she wanted. If Pfizer wanted to put tapeworm eggs into pill form, surely they could figure out how to do it without my permission.

She took her hand off my leg. "Let me get to the point, sweetheart. We'd like your co-operation. We've got some questions about genetics. We need to find Mr. Ishimoto. We'd like to borrow some worms. He seems to have vanished into the woodwork. And because I like you, Mr. Noir — I like you a lot — and I mean that — I'm honor bound to tell you that Pfizer has some rough people working for it. We're not all English majors, darling. Some of our people got an MFA in the art of nasty. There are medications that can turn very nice people into bloodsucking fiends with shaved heads and mirror shades who get a kick out of scaring people into involuntary bowel movements. Men with no family, no friends, who spend their nights at the gym and do three hundred crunches at a sitting and then four hundred push-ups. Men who are programmed to attack on command."

She made a good case — that Pfizer needed the tapeworm queens and was willing to unleash the dogs of war to get it. I saw no need to tell her that the queens were bad queens and that they were gone, probably in the possession of the Bogus Brothers. I could still make a deal, sell the worms to Scarlett, avoid being pounded to a pulp, walk away with a bundle, and then disappear before Pfizer was any the wiser. Why not? Naomi had two best-selling books and a booming business in China. She was out in the Milky Way somewhere, circling the Pleiades. I ran a daily Google search on her, and she was here, there, and everywhere talking about *The Blessing of Less* as the answer to all of mankind's problems — it and its sequel, *The Loss of Austerity,* sold like iced lemonade in Hades — and she bought herself an eighteen-room apartment in a co-op on Fifth Avenue so exclusive that the Dalai Lama had been turned down by the co-op board, and so had Toni Morrison, Archbishop Tutu, Mr. Rogers, and Elie Wiesel. I called Naomi's number over and over and over and got a personal assistant — a different one each time — Anna, Brianna, Arianna, Madison, Addison, Natalie, Destiny, Brooklyn — *Brooklyn??* Yes, Brooklyn. A twenty-two-year-old with a breathy voice, drop-dead polite, like all of them, and she had *no idea* where Naomi was or who I was or why, and she wrote down all my information, as did Anna, Brianna, Arianna, et al. — slips of paper accumulated with my name and number on them, and no call from Naomi.

So I was on my own.

Pfizer did not believe in Lessness. I knew that much. It had earned gazillions from Viagra and from a super form of Viagra called Biagra that gives a man an erection for eight to ten hours and that nursing homes and hospitals gave to old men at night to keep them from rolling out of bed. And then there was Niagra for urinary tract problems, which makes an old man piss like a palomino. And Miagra, a pacifier that calms anxiety and also induces forgetfulness, so you are likely to take all of your pills a second or third time, thus giving Pfizer sales a nice boost. If Pfizer wanted to hire a couple of shooters to ding my bell, they had the dough to do it. If they could grease the skids for that $200 billion federal giveaway to the big pharms in the Medicare drug program — the day Congress put all of its principles into cold storage and promised to pay *full retail price* for Gamma and Gampy's Lipitor and not negotiate a deal — then Pfizer could handle an old gumshoe like me.

I rubbed my nose. I tugged on my chin. I looked out the window and crossed and

211

uncrossed my legs. It didn't take me long to decide to capitulate. I said, softly, "I can get you a worm. Do you want it dead or alive?"

"Either one works for us."

"Give me an hour, and I'll have what you want," I said. We shook hands. She ordered a BLT and an extra-large latte. She intended to stay right there.

# 17
## Mr. Banana Comes to Town

I went upstairs to my devastated office and looked around in the drifts of debris for the envelope with the death pills. Larry B. Larry's goons had pulled handfuls of papers from the drawers and flung them every which way, and you know? If someone had stuck a radio transmitter in my scrotum, I might've been out for revenge, too. I searched through the mess, and as I did, it occurred to me that (1) I was never going to return to the twelfth floor of the Acme Building and (2) I was not going to miss the old dump much. What a misspent life. A 1978 calendar from Sam's Clam Disco. A poster for *Splendor in the Grass* starring Natalie Wood and Warren Beatty. A pink boa, a souvenir of some party, a vague memory in a cloud of gin, and a pink polka-dot hanky, probably from the same party. A box of matchbooks from the Capriccio Hotel in Vegas. An ad for comedian Eddie

Rictus at the Can Can Casino. Some old detective paperbacks: *The Blonde in 204, Close Cover Before Striking, Dead Men Don't Shop.* A wall plaque, glass broken: IT'S BETTER TO GO OUT BURNISHED FROM USE THAN RUSTING FROM PRINCIPLE. A bronzed fruitcake, courtesy of Thompson Tooth Tinsel. A newspaper story on a survey that showed that the rate of infidelity among women named Evelyn is very low. A sheet of coupons good for 25 percent off at the Hat Hut. A black sweatshirt that said, GO AHEAD, ASK ME. THE ANSWER IS YES. A recipe for The Seven Joys of General Tsao Chicken Almond Ding. A paper fan with a picture of Charles Wesley and underneath "Epworth League, Seward, Nebraska." Two tickets to the Schoolbus Demolition Derby at the Minnesota State Fair. From some catalog, a picture of a girl in a skimpy outfit: "Our shimmering silky flip skirt will make you the belle of the ball, especially topped off with our oh-so-naughty lace tee, festooned with hand embroidered butterflies."

And the picture of Nevaeh in the Pontiac. Ah, Nevaeh. *Why did you do it? Thank you for doing it. You shouldn't have done it. What are you doing to me?*

I didn't hear the footsteps in the hall.

214

"Hey, Numb Nuts. Wake up and die right."

It was Lieutenant McCafferty in the doorway, in his customary green plaid jacket and porkpie hat, the bulge under the left arm. He looked around at the devastation. "Looks like you survived a tornado, Noir. Consider yourself lucky." He kicked a pile of folders aside and plopped down in my client chair. "Gimme a shot of your whiskey," he said, and I dug out the bottle from the bottom file drawer and found a Dixie cup and poured him a shot. "I been dealing with losers all day, I need a little elegance in my life. Ignorance and cruelty and greed, that's my daily diet. This morning I hadda deal with a little punk who shoved his grandma down the stairs. Two flights. Old lady in a print dress, hair up in a bun, lying there at the bottom of the stairs, two minutes after she'd made him breakfast. Eggs and cottage fries and bacon. Eggs over easy. He wanted sunny-side up. So boom, down the stairs she went."

He gave me a long, lingering look. "Hey, you look pretty good, buddy boy. I hear the ladies are climbing all over you."

"I've been working out and watching my diet, lieutenant."

He snorted. "Hell you have. You've been

215

ingesting illegal drugs, and you've been selling them on the open market. You got Bac-O Bits for brains, buddy boy. And you're in more trouble than you ever thought possible. You ever hear of Johnny Banana?"

"*The* Johnny Banana?"

"There is but one. The capo del capo del grande primo capo. And also the recto del recto del recto del humungo recto, if you're up on your Italian. He came to town looking for you, buddy boy. He's up in the penthouse suite at the St. Paul Hotel, with ten pinstripe guys the size of refrigerators, and he's sitting and tapping his foot and chewing on his cigar, and he's saying your name under his breath over and over. The word is out: you're a marked man. These boys aren't playing tiddlywinks. They want you bad, and when they get you, they're gonna squeeze you hard, and then they're gonna include you in some construction project."

"Does Joey know about this?"

The lieutenant laughed. "Joey is a sardine. When the killer shark comes on the scene, the sardines find a rock to hide under."

"What does he want?"

"You, buddy boy. He wants you."

"I may need your protection, Lieutenant."

McCafferty chuckled. "Lots of people maybe need my protection, Noir. Fourteen-year-old girls out on their first dates may need my protection, and folks purchasing a home unaware of the plumbing problems, and folks who leave the potato salad sitting in the sun too long, and maybe someone has taken too big a bite of porterhouse steak and isn't chewing it properly, but we can't protect everybody, can we? Somewhere this very minute a blind man may be crossing a busy street against a red light. Somewhere there are oily rags close to a frayed extension cord. I'm not Clark Kent, pal."

I mentioned to him that as a peace officer, he had an obligation, and he held up his hand — "I don't know nothing about it, Noir, and I wasn't here, and anybody who says so is a liar." And he finished his whiskey and upped and left. The door clicked shut, and my heart jumped. It sounded like the hammer of a gun.

I sat in my office, and I tried to scope out a plan. Nuts to Scarlett and Pfizer. I'd clean out my savings account and head north. Birch had a cabin on Lake Watab near Avon. I could cool my heels in the woods and catch up on my reading and wait for Mr. Banana to get bored and go away. I removed a couple ceiling tiles where I'd stashed a hundred packs of Elongate and my old .38 snub-nosed revolver and a box of shells, and I fished my Rolodex out of the debris and dropped it all in a Dayton's shopping bag, and then my phone rang. UNKNOWN CALLER, it said on the screen. A second ring. ANSWER THE PHONE, it said. A third ring. HEAR ME, MR. NOIR?? So I clicked *answer.*

A voice at the other end sounded like a load of gravel sliding down a chute. "Mr. Noir, this is Johnny. Johnny Banana. I'd like to meet with you. Right away." It was the voice of a man who's been drinking whiskey on a daily basis with battery acid for a chaser and smoking acetylene cigarettes. If concrete blocks could talk, they'd sound like that voice.

"What a pleasant surprise," I said. "I was hoping you had come to town to see me. It's been a long time, sir."

"A long time since what?"

"We met once before. In Chicago. At Benny's."

I was lying through my ears. Also I was sneaking down the stairs as tippy-toe as possible toward where my car was parked, in the alley by the back door to Nacho Mama.

"Benny?" he said. "Benny who?"

"Well, he went by a whole bunch of names."

"You mean Benny Brunello?"

"Yeah. The big guy. With the eyebrows. Right?"

I was in the alley now and putting the key in the car door.

"What's that sound?" he said. "You on your way somewhere?"

"On my way to wherever you want to meet," I said. "But you better hurry because my battery is about to die. In fact, I think —" And I clicked off the cell phone. I got in the car and raced onto I-94 heading north toward Avon. Traffic was light through the Loring Tunnel and past the Basilica of St. Mary. I had six grand on me. I wondered if I should go back to the bank and get more. I got off the freeway and circled around behind the basilica to meditate on what to do. It's a big basilica, and it casts a long shadow. I punched in Birch's number on the phone and was about to call her and ask where the key to the cabin was hidden — *on the porch, under a bait bucket,* I thought — and there was no answer. *Naomi.* I dialed her number, and — a miracle! — she answered. *"Namaste,"* she said. I heard water bubbling in the background and women ululating, accompanied by drums and tiny bells.

"*Namaste* yourself, babes. This is your security man, and I am about to go into a permanent weight-loss program, the kind you do underground in a narrow wooden box."

"I can't deal with this right now."

"You can't? Well, think how I feel."

She was at a spa in the Adirondacks called Serenity Springs. Lying in a hot mineral bath while someone named Jorge massaged her face with mint leaves. He was whispering something to her, something about leaving all anxiety and conflictedness behind.

"My yoga session is at two. I'll call you afterward," she said in a serene voice.

"There is no afterward. Afterward doesn't exist. Serenity is not applicable here. I'm in deep trouble, kid. My little boat is drifting toward Niagara, I need to get ashore."

She sighed. "I wish you the inner peace of a harmonious heart," she said. And then she said, "Oh, wow." And then dial tone. I pulled out of the basilica parking lot and back onto I-94 and put the pedal to the metal, thinking about Birch's little cabin in the pines, also estimating how long I could live on six thousand dollars. And then I saw movement in the rearview mirror, and a man's voice behind me said, "Easy does it,

Mr. Noir. Let's pull off at the next exit and have us a little conversation."

I took the Dowling exit and drove west to Crystal Lake cemetery and drove in, slowly, and stopped next to a statue of a weeping angel and a headstone that said, BELOW THIS HUMBLE MONUMENT THERE LIES, MUZZLED WITH DUST, HER SOUL IN PARADISE, OUR CHERISHED DAUGHTER QUICKLY FLED TO THE IMMORTAL LIVING FROM THE DEAD. CORINNE.

The man in the backseat slipped slowly out of the car and stood by my window for a moment and then strolled around the front of the car and opened the door and sat in the shotgun seat. He was short and plump, with moisturized skin and caramelized hair, in a black short-sleeve silk shirt and black spangly pants, skintight, and sandals with tassels. If he was packing a gun, he had concealed it awfully well. He smelled of an exotic fragrance, sweet and lemony, and he smiled an insincere smile. "I'm Cliff Kress, chief acceptance officer, Food and Drug Administration in Washington, D. C. It's a pleasure to finally meet you, Mr. Noir." He snapped open his billfold and flashed an ID with a gold seal on it.

"What a coincidence. I was just about to

call you, Mr. Kress."

He shook his head, as if I had said something very dumb. "Please spare me the persiflage, Mr. Noir. I'm not in the mood."

I pressed on. "I have so much I want to tell you, Mr. Kress. I don't know where to start."

"Let's start with you shutting up," he said. I could see by his bemused expression that he was onto me. He looked like Miss Mac-Donald looked when I told her I had forgotten my book report on the bus.

"I am a private investigator, Mr. Kress, and I've been working undercover trying to get the goods on these shysters who are selling parasites to the American people. And I finally have succeeded in tracing the chain of command up to Mr. Big. An old man named Joey. And he asked me to make you an offer. One hundred thousand-dollar bills, the ones with Mr. Grover Cleveland on them. We can have them in your hands by tomorrow morning. Nine a.m."

"I'm not for sale. Been bought already." He laughed a hard, worldly laugh.

"Mr. Noir, you and I are grown men. Let's not waste time playing footsie. You're selling a drug called Elongate. You're earning a lot of money from it. Uncle Sam doesn't like it when you put a drug out there without asking permission. The FDA has lawyers who practically come to climax at the thought of prosecuting people like yourself."

I was about to say something about the presumption of innocence, and he held up his hand. "Hear me out, Mr. Noir. It's not what you think it is." He reached over and switched on the radio.

"Just in case your car is bugged, sir."

It was a jazz station. A breathy woman sang:

> I get no kick from cocaine.
> Mere crystal meth doesn't take away my
>     breath
> But kick me, darling, please do
> And I'll get a kick out of you.

Mr. Kress leaned over and said in a quiet voice: "I'm retiring from the FDA in three weeks, Mr. Noir. And I'm taking a job with Pfizer. I'm leaving public service at $71,000 a year, and I'm joining Pfizer for $385,000 a year. Not a difficult decision. So I guess you can figure out why I'm here. Two months ago, my friends at Pfizer would've been happy to negotiate a deal with you, but the time for talk has passed, Mr. Noir. You stood up Scarlett Anderson an hour ago. That wasn't very smart of you."

"I went up to my office to get the stuff she asked for and someone had trashed the place."

He reached into his back pocket and pulled out a folded paper.

"Just sign this, Mr. Noir, and your troubles are over."

I glanced at the paper. It seemed to be a transfer of all rights pertaining to Elongate or any weight-loss product whatsoever.

"What about Naomi? What about Mr. Ishimoto?"

"They've signed it already."

"What about Johnny Banana?"

Mr. Kress turned a slight shade of pale. "What about Johnny Banana?" The name set off Mr. Kress's internal alarm system, no doubt about it. Very interesting.

"I just sold him my interest in Elongate this morning. I've got his number here if you want to call it." I lied in a calm business-like tone, the way a person is supposed to. I scrolled up the call register and gave him McCafferty's number.

I couldn't tell if Mr. Kress was buying the story or not. "I'll get back to you," he said. He turned the radio off and pulled out his cell phone and pressed a button, and a minute later I could hear a helicopter descending. It landed about fifty yards away, and he walked to it and climbed in. On the fuselage it said: PFIZER. And up it went into the sky, the air pounding with the beat of the rotors until it disappeared beyond the river, heading east.

He hadn't told me to wait around so I didn't. I turned the car around and headed toward St. Paul on I-94. There would be no Avon for me until I could reach Naomi. I was 100 percent sure she had signed no transfer of rights whatsoever. Well, I was 85 percent sure — anyone who had written a book called *The Blessing of Less* was conceivably capable of throwing away a fortune. I called Mr. Ishimoto, and he denied having signed a paper for Mr. Kress. His voice sounded odd on the phone, though. Like maybe someone had a loop of piano wire around his neck.

"Is someone holding a gun to your head right now, Mr. Ishimoto? If the answer is yes, say 'I don't know.' "

"I don't know," he said.

"And is it a bunch of guys in pinstriped suits, and is one of them named Johnny Banana?"

"I don't know."

"And have they found the worms, sir?"

"I know," he said.

"You're sure they haven't?"

"Positive."

"Good luck, Mr. Ishimoto."

"I don't know," he said. "Maybe." And then the line went dead.

I had a weak moment right then. Panic made me do it. I gave Lieutenant McCafferty a jingle and told him that an armed killer was after me and what was he going to do about it. I pleaded for my life. He was unmoved. "It's a jungle and there's not much I can do, Noir. You can't keep the cougars from hunting the deer. Violence is part of life. The mouse is in the cornfield, shopping for his family, and suddenly there is a rush of owl wings, and he feels a sting in his back, and then he is very high in the air. The vultures and jackals who wait for their dinner to die a natural death before they move in are not the animals we admire. The killers are the ones we name our football teams after. I didn't make the world, Noir. I just enjoy looking at it."

I pulled off the freeway onto the road that ran along the Mississippi and pulled into an overlook under the Franklin Avenue bridge, its great concrete arches leaping the river gorge. A tow of eight empty barges plowed two abreast downstream, riding high in the water, pushed by the tug, its big engines hammering *whump whump whump.* The nameplate on the pilothouse said, WHIT-NEY MACMILLAN. A deckhand stood in an open door, a young dude, shirtless, smoking a cigarette. Suddenly I wanted to be him, watching the world go by, the houses on the leafy bluff, the cars in the long driveways, the patient daddies on their rider mowers, knowing that none of it pertained to me, feeling the liberty of the great waterway. Minnesota suddenly seemed less hospitable to me. I had ended a pleasant interlude and now had come to a plateau from which one descends into the deep, cold valley of re-ality. There, attempting to cross a bridge into the future, I would encounter an ugly troll who would seize my billfold and chase me down a road paved with bricks of sor-row that leads to a cliff, and I would fall off it and hit the ground and be old and fat and misunderstood — and life would go on as it had before, except even more so. *Un-less* I could make a bold leap now — like the dude on the deck. Fly to New York. Rent a car. Drive to Southampton and find Naomi and the Rama Lama Monongahela before they could fly off to Paris together.

Better yet, get over to Mr. Ishimoto's and go head to head with Johnny Banana and his pinstriped goons. *Hey you. Banana.*

*Looky here. It's Noir, calling your bluff, Man with Fruit Name. Put up or shut up.* The way to deal with brutes and bullies is to poke 'em in the snoot. Subtlety and subterfuge don't work. Pull up your jockstrap and walk up to the big bruiser and give him what for. He's expecting you to wheedle and whimper, and instead you sock him in the beezer, *whammo.* Shock and awe.

*That's what a Noir would do,* said a still small voice. *When did a Noir ever back away from a fight?*

The still small voice didn't know my family very well. The still small voice was ignorant of the facts. We've been dodging fights ever since Great-Grandpa William Tecumseh Noir waltzed away from the draft in 1917. His older brother Robert E. Noir was a steward aboard the RMS *Titanic* and leaped into the first lifeboat, wearing a lady's wig and a shawl, elbowing aside small children. Ulysses S. Noir collected wristwatches off the bodies of investors who leaped from high windows on Wall Street after the Crash of 1929, and though the watches were broken and the hands stuck at the time of impact, he tried to sell them at full price twenty-four hours later. His son, Stonewall Noir, was an airman at Pearl Harbor that December morning and pedaled his bike away from the burning buildings as fast as he could and took shelter in a joint called Honolulu Lou's and got drunk and fell off his bike on the way back to the base and was awarded the Purple Heart. Audie Noir had a sore throat on D-day and went to the infirmary rather than go ashore at Normandy and lay in bed sucking cream soda through a straw. George S. Noir named names to the McCarthy committee in 1953, some of them Communists, some Methodists. Douglas Noir was drafted during the Korean conflict, and aboard the troopship to Seoul he suddenly started weeping and babbling and tearing his hair out, which other men did, too, but he did it with more force and conviction and was declared unfit to serve due to mental instability and girlish tendencies and was sent back to Texas, where he resumed his studies in chiropractic. Omar Noir was a physicist at Los Alamos and fell in love with a waitress named Natasha, who turned out to be a Soviet agent and asked him to turn over nuclear secrets, and he said, "Do that again what you did a moment ago, and I'll start writing out formulas." Uncle Dwight D. Noir commandeered a chopper and flew solo away from the American embassy in Saigon as the city fell in April 1975, and flew to Bali and treated himself to three weeks at a luxury resort with money he'd embezzled from the USO.

So in keeping with family tradition, I gave up the fight. I stopped at the bank and cleaned out my account — "What's her name, Mr. Noir?" said Charlene. "Who's the lucky girl you're going to Paris with?" — and hustled over to St. John the Lesser Episcopal Church on Wacouta Street to beg for sanctuary.

# 18
## THE MOTHER CHURCH

I knew the rector, Father Bert Smalley, from the Five Spot. He was a thirsty man. He liked vodka martinis. Sanctity is hard work for low pay, and after a long day of reverence, Father Bert liked to stroll in and put a quarter in the jukebox and belly up to the bar and toss down two martinis in succession as the Revelators sang:

*Why do men act that way*
*And break our hearts every day*
*Why do we bother to love?*

*Men wear their pants down low*
*Playing with their video*
*Why do we bother to love?*

*Why do they lie to you*
*And say I do when it isn't true.*
*I love them cause I know I should*
*But I know they're no darn good.*

And he sat chewing the olives and ordered

his third martini, the one that loosened his tongue, and he'd start babbling about the sorrows of his life, the uncertainty of his calling, his faith journey, blah blah blah.

It was an odd parish, St. John the Lesser. A gray stone Cass Gilbert castle on a block jammed with bars and pawnshops, a church with a tiny congregation, mostly gays and lesbians, and an enormous endowment, thanks to a horse farm bequeathed to it by the late Brewster Wylie (of Wylie, Warburton & Wordsworth). The farm had been subdivided and planted with mansionettes, and the millions in revenue enabled St. John the Lesser to put on the dog in a big way. The gays and lesbians were radical in politics and conservative in liturgy, and every Sunday morning the place was aswirl with cassocks, chasubles, albs, and surplices — and not army surplus surplices but fancy silk, gold-embroidered, with Italian cinctures — a flock of acolytes bearing a six-foot cross and candles and an embroidered banner (*Veni, Creator*), a tall black woman with shaved head and shining raiment swinging a censer like a house afire, smoke billowing up, and another woman with a crew cut flinging holy water from a silver tube — and bringing up the rear, the great mass of Father Smalley, his alb swishing, genuflecting grandly, hurling blessings left and right, as the choir of men and boys in starched ruffled collars chanted seventeenth-century plainsong. Henry VIII would have been quite comfortable attending mass at St. John, except for the homily, which tended to call for revolution and the overthrow of the privileged classes, including (presumably) Brewster Wylie, their great benefactor.

I found Father Bert in his office, listening to a jazz quintet play the bejesus out of "Caravan," and I described my predicament. He was a fan of detective novels, and he was intrigued when I told him about Johnny Banana dogging my trail. I told him I needed to take sanctuary in his sanctuary, and he said, "Oh, that is thrilling. What an opportunity for grace." He ran around poking into closets, and soon I was enveloped in a black woolen cassock with hood and leather sandals and a pectoral cross the size of a fence post. "You hit someone with that, and they're gonna get visions," said Father. He led me off behind a statue of the archangel Michael, arms outstretched as if pleading with an umpire, to a small, windowless room off the vestry. There was a black leather couch and a low table piled with Sunday bulletins. "This is the acolytes' lounge," he said. "You can bed down here for the night, and we'll work out a long-term plan tomorrow. There's a retreat center up in Bemidji. You could go there, but you'd be expected to spend four hours a day in prayer." He handed me a couple fat cigars, a snifter of brandy, some dark chocolates, and a can of Mace. "If the sons of bitches come in the night, brain them with the cross and squirt some Mace in their faces. That'll slow 'em down." For a man of God, he seemed quite enthused about violence. "I wouldn't mind sticking around and duking it out with them myself, but I have to go visit a parishioner in the morning who's getting a new kidney. But if you ring this buzzer" — he pointed to a button by the couch — "I'll hear it and come down and kick the crap out of them. By the way, what are they all riled up about?"

"I've got something they want. A magic formula for weight loss."

Father Smalley's eyes widened. "Lord have mercy. An answer to prayer. Where can I get some?"

I handed him a little capsule, and he opened his mouth and down it went. "What sort of diet do I have to go on?"

"Meat and potatoes. All you like. They love pot roast."

"They?"

"The tapeworms."

He gave me an inquiring look and then grinned and chuckled. "You're a funny man, Mr. Noir. A funny, funny man."

It is spooky, trying to drift off to sleep in an empty church. In a crowded church on Christmas Eve, listening to the sermon about how we should observe the Nativity every day of the year in our hearts, sleep comes easily, but in a little room off a big empty sanctuary, lights out, I lay for an hour, turning and tossing. I tried to think positive thoughts. I tried to imagine Marvin telling me I now had a net worth of a million dollars. I visualized my slender self in a red thong swimsuit, my proud glutes glistening in the sun as I strode out onto the diving board at the Minikahda Club. I wanted to be rich so as to free myself from envy, that creepy sin, and the greenish yearning to be cool and go to an Ivy school and not have to think about money. The Kennedy brothers were so cool, they walked around without money in their pockets, knowing that when the waiter brought the check, someone less cool would pay. Midwesterners envy the coastal people who seem not so inhibited by modesty and all the clunky moral baggage. I know better than to envy New Yorkers, being one myself and having ridden the subway all those years, but I envy a flannel-brain writer I know who wrote a TV sitcom pilot in which unattractive people throw insults at each other, and every sixty seconds there is a double take and a slow burn. He hired me to sit in cafés and write down dialogue that I heard. The sitcom got made, and he, without ever having to write another word, got a sliver of the profits, which turned out to be vast, and so he lives in a twelve-room co-op apartment on Riverside Drive with umber tile floors and rattan carpets and antique French country furniture and jets off to Paris or Peru when he likes and has more fun than I do, seeing as how I spend so much time wishing he would get Lyme disease so I could visit him in the nursing home and bring him flowers.

I lay imagining his misery, his remorse, listening to the hum of cars on the interstate nearby, and I detected some clinking and clacking not so far away. And then clicking. A definite clicking in the shadows. A series of sharp clicks, and then a whiff of perfume, and then a shadowy figure leaning over me, and a low seductive voice said, "Guy, I came to see that you're all right."

"Who's there?"

"Chanterelle is my name. I'm a huge fan of yours. I've always wanted to meet you. This is so exciting for me."

There was a sort of vibrato in her voice, a warble in the midrange, that normally you only hear in movies, the throb of womanly desire. I reached out and touched a bare leg.

"I don't believe I know a Chanterelle," I said.

"You will, in just a moment. Is there room on that couch for me?" she said. I said that I didn't think there was. "Then I'll just lie on top of you," she said.

And then she did.

She was not heavy at all, I noticed. And also, she was buck naked. My hands traced her bare back, which was long and beautifully curved and led to majestic buttocks whose firmness suggested a regular exercise regimen. "Are you surprised?" she said.

"Astonished. How'd you get in?"

"Knock and it shall be opened unto you."

She kissed my neck and unfastened my cassock. "I never made love with a man of the cloth before," she murmured. "Have you taken vows or anything?"

I shook my head.

"Are you a believer?"

"I wasn't one before you came in, darling, and now I'm seriously reconsidering."

"Are you Episcopalian?"

"I could be. What about you, darling? I want to believe what you believe."

She lay there, naked, breathing on my cheek. "Well," she said, "what I was brought up to believe was that God had revealed Himself to us Southern Baptists and not to anyone else. The others were barbarians and we were God's chosen, and so if we beat up on them, we were carrying out God's will. But then I became a dancer, and now I believe that God has given all these wonderful gifts for us to share with others, no matter who they are or what they believe. Gifts like the human body, which is beautiful. Don't you think?

"I couldn't agree more."

"I think that God is getting ready to bless you real good, Brother Guy." She arose to remove my clothing, and in the faint glow from the open door and the stained-glass window of a tall bearded guy holding a sheep, I caught the silhouette of her bountiful breasts, each one a beauty, so firm, so fully formed, it was hard to pick a favorite. She was a marble goddess who stepped down off a pedestal and became flesh, a goddess of life's generosity, with curly black tendrils like licorice candy on her head and a tattoo of an orchid on her lower belly and broad child-bearing hips and thighs so white you could've eaten off them. She removed the cross from my pectorals. "You have excellent taste in crosses," she said. She clunked it down on the floor. I could tell by the careless way she handled it that she hadn't been brought up Catholic. "Don't you worry about a thing, darling," she said, and her tone of voice told me that something worrisome was just about to happen. You develop an ear for falsehood in this line of work. Oddly, at the moment, I did not care that she was part of something treacherous. She took the hem of the cassock and raised it and caressed my rib cage and slipped my jockeys off. "All ready to go, I see," she said. She said that she had never met anyone so manly as I, and she asked me what sort of things I liked, and would it be okay if she went to the little girls' room and peed, and then a low, gravelly voice said, "You know why you can't hear a pterodactyl go to the bathroom? Because the P is silent." And a big, hairy arm wrapped around my throat, and I felt the cold barrel of a pistol press against my temple. "Sorry to break up the party, but it's time to talk, Noir," said the low, gravelly voice, which of course I remembered from the telephone. "So let's get up and talk. Beat it, babes."

The girl got off me. "I'm going, Johnny, I'm going." She put a hand on my cheek. " 'Bye, sweetie. You take care now. I'm sorry I didn't get the chance to like you as much as I'm sure I could." She ducked out the door, and her high heels went *klikklikklik* across the marble floor. A young woman with magnificent buttocks walking buck naked into the sacristy and past the choir stalls of St. John the Lesser. An image to conjure with, except that Mr. Banana was pressing the barrel rather firmly into my temple.

"Stand up nice and slow," he said, "and nobody gets hurt."

I stood up and covered myself with the cassock. My maleness, which had been at attention a few seconds before, now hung flaccid, which, I suppose, is perfectly natural when you are about to be shot in the head. I looked at Mr. Banana and chuckled.

"What's so funny?" he said.

"That line, 'Stand up nice and slow and nobody gets hurt.' You been watching old Richard Widmark movies? You been reading Dick Tracy in the funny pages? What a letdown. I figured that when you nabbed

240

me and bumped me off, at least it'd be done with style and a modicum of originality. I suppose there's only so many ways of saying 'Stick 'em up,' but still."

He jabbed me with the pistol. "Shuddup, you. When I want your literary opinion, I'll ask for it," he growled. But I could tell that I had struck a nerve. He nodded toward the door and shoved the pistol into my back, but his brow was furrowed, he was thinking over the line about standing up nice and slow and nobody gets hurt, rewriting it. Johnny Banana is no small-time street punk, he is a capo del capo del grande primo capo, and as such he naturally wants to walk and talk with a grand style that is his and his alone, not employ worn-out clichés, same as he wouldn't go around in threads he got from a Goodwill store or drive an old beater of a car or order beans and wieners at a café. He pushed me out the door and past the high altar, a single candle flickering on it, and down past the choir stalls and down the steps into the sanctuary, and then he stopped.

"So what would you have said if you were me, smart guy?" he growled.

I pondered that. "I would've said, 'One false move out of you, and I'm gonna fill you with more holes than a slice of Swiss cheese.' "

"Ha! That's even worse than 'Stand up nice and slow and nobody gets hurt,' " he said. "You don't know what you're talking about, crum bum."

I said, "I was pulling your leg — how about this? 'Rise and shine, boy-o, and don't be reaching for anything except air.' "

"That's better," he said. "But I don't know about 'boy-o.' I ain't Irish."

"Okay, then. Try this. 'On your feet, pal. And if I see any sudden moves, you're going to be suddenly dead.' "

He shook his head. "Don't sound right. There's no rhythm to it."

"Okay, I got it. This is good. 'Time for the recessional, choirboy. And say a prayer that my trigger finger don't slip and send you skidding into the hereafter.' "

He said it to himself, under his breath. "I like it," he said. " 'Recessional' is good, and 'skidding into the hereafter' — very cool." He pointed to a pew. "Siddown." I sat. He stuck the gun in my mug and said, "Time for the recessional, choirboy." He said it again. "I like it," he said. "Except for the trigger finger. That doesn't sound like me."

"How about 'And say a prayer that my gun don't go boom and make your skull a part of the real estate'?"

"I like 'skidding into the hereafter' better."

I nodded. He drew himself up to full height: "Time for the recessional, choirboy. And say a prayer that my gun don't go boom and send you skidding into the hereafter." He said it again. And a third time. Johnny Banana was, like any other capo del capo del grande primo capo, a true stylist. I could see that, looking at his pegged pants with the sharp creases, the spotless white tie against the black shirt, the padded shoulders of his silver jacket, the perfect crest of his pompadour.

"I don't know about 'skidding into the hereafter,'" he said. "I liked it at first, and now I'm not sure."

"How about 'flapping into the hereafter'?"

"I don't know. Let me hear you say it."

"You want me to say it?"

"Yeah. Say it."

"Wouldn't make any sense coming from me. You're the one with the heater."

"Here." He handed me his pistol.

"Sit down," I said. "I can't get the right feel for it with you standing there."

So he sat down in the pew.

"Actually," I said, "I think it'd be more realistic if you kneel."

"I just want to hear the line," he said.

"I gotta feel it before I can say it," I said. "I want to say it with conviction."

So he pulled out a kneeler and knelt on it, as if in prayer, leaning forward over the back of the pew in front.

"I gotta have a motivation," I said. "What's the story?"

"Imagine that you caught me welshing on a deal, and you came to find me, and there I was in church, naked, about to stick it to my girlfriend, Chanterelle, and that's when you pulled the gun on me," he said.

"You dirty rat," I said, and I conked him a good hard one on the noggin, and he toppled over, and his head bounced off the arm of the pew, and he lay crumpled in the aisle, getting his nice suit wrinkled. Johnny Banana, Mr. Big himself, toppled in the sanctuary of St. John the Lesser, saliva trickling out of a corner of his mouth.

I poked him with my toe and said, "How quickly the tables turn, banana brain. Vanity goeth before a fall, and so forth and so on."

I stuck the pectoral cross in Mr. Banana's limp paw and called Lieutenant McCafferty and told him I'd gone to church for early mass and caught someone stealing a crucifix and could he come right away, and then I called up Gene Williker and said, "Big scoop, pal," and told him, and called Boyd

Freud, and then I slipped out the side door and spotted a black car, motor idling, the lights on, four goons in pinstripes inside it with headphones on, heads bouncing to the beat of different drummers, and I stuffed a wad of cardboard up the tailpipe, and a couple minutes later, up comes McCafferty in the squad car and peels to a stop and jumps out to find the goons in dreamland from carbon monoxide and Johnny Banana staggering out the church door with a cross in his hand, bleeding from where I had whopped him. He stood in the entrance, swaying like a tall spruce in a high wind. "You'll never take me alive, copper," he said, and McCafferty snapped the cuffs on him and then spotted me.

"What you looking at, Noir?" he said. "You involved in this? If you are, I got an extra pair of cuffs in the car."

"Just out for a walk in my cassock, and I stopped to admire the fine police work," I said. "I'd offer to lend a hand, but it looks like you got it under control. Remind me to drop a note to Mayor Coleman and tell him that when the chiefship comes open, there's no need to look outside the department." McCafferty shrugged and went to call for reinforcements. Mr. Banana gave me a ferocious and baleful look. It would've been more ferocious, but his eye was starting to swell shut from where he'd hit his head. "I'll get you, Noir, if it's the last thing I do," he growled.

"Johnny," I said. "I don't mean to put words in your mouth, but the press will be on the scene shortly, and you want to make a good impression. Now you could say something rough and mean, like 'I'll be on a plane and out of this stinkin' town before you guys have another cuppa coffee.' Or you could go for a humorous touch — something like 'Well, looky who showed up at the party. What's the matter, boys? Ain't you ever seen a man in bracelets before?' Or how about 'Tell my muddah I ain't never going to early Mass again'?"

Mr. Banana pondered these possibilities. "What's wrong with 'I'll get you if it's the last thing I do'?"

"Johnny," I said. "As a friend, I got to tell you, that is a horseshit line. Number one, it's craven and mealy-mouthed, and number two, people don't know who I am. It's Banana they know. Noir they never heard of. It's like Richard Nixon blaming a stenographer for Watergate. Think big, Johnny."

"Think big?"

I whispered the phrase in his ear. And up rolled the paddy wagon, and six cops jumped out and, ten seconds later, Gene Willikers and his photographer Flash Flanagan, who was jumping around like crazy, his Speed Graphic going *kachik kachik kachik kachik,* snapping McCafferty, who stood patiently in an aggressive law-enforcement pose, right hand on his pistol handle, left hand on his hip, hat at a rakish angle, a stern but judicious and slightly jaded expression on his face, as if he were weary of all the attention and acclaim.

Johnny faced the camera and said, "You think you got Johnny Banana, but all you got is a handful of shadows. I'll be out of this stinking town before you guys" — and then he forgot the line — "before you guys" — he looked around for me — "before you guys get your second cup of coffee and a jelly doughnut." He looked grandly contemptuous, just as a top-level mobster should look, curled lip and all. And then Boyd Freud wheeled up in the Channel 5 news-mobile, and McCafferty had to wait for the newsman to unbundle his camera and a portable floodlight and a microphone, and when he finally had the camera on his shoulder, McCafferty uncuffed Johnny Banana and hauled him back into the church, and when Boyd yelled "Action!"

the detective walked the perp down the steps.

"Any comment, Mr. Banana?" said Boyd.

"I already said what I had to say."

"Okay, but I didn't get it on tape."

Johnny thought for a moment. "By the time you guys get out of this stinking town, I'll be on my third cup of coffee. Tell my mother I'll be home for lunch," he said. Not a bad line at all. McCafferty recuffed him and said, "Watch your head, Banana," and shoved him into the back of the squad car.

Gene asked me what happened, and I said, "Gene, it was ace police work, top to bottom. I was a block away, out for a walk, and heard a scuffle and saw McCafferty overpower the five of them single-handed, and by the time I arrived on the scene, the show was over."

"Can I quote you?"

"Not by name," I said. "I don't want to steal the lieutenant's spotlight."

"You've lost weight," he said. "You have some sort of wasting disease? Should we be updating the obituary?"

"Ask my girlfriends," I said. "I keep three of them busy seven days a week."

"I hear you moved to Minneapolis."

"A weekend place," I said. "I'm a St. Paul boy. There is no place like home."

# 19
## EPILOGUE, I GUESS

I walked away from the scene, the red and blue lights flashing, into the dark night of downtown St. Paul. Not much nightlife at two a.m. People poop out around ten or eleven, and the young have flown to look for trouble in Minneapolis. My car was parked in a lot around there somewhere. I walked up the alley behind Robert's Ready-to-Wear and Closets R Us and Alpine Recliners and spotted a shadowy figure knocking on the stage door of the Fitzgerald Theater in a hopeless, furtive way. He wore faded jeans and red shoes and red socks and a maroon jacket with a big *A* on it and ANOKA TORNADOES.

I tapped him on the shoulder. "The show's not here tonight, pal. It's in New York this month."

He turned, and I recognized him as the show's old announcer, the one who read the commercials for duct tape and cat food and baked products. His enormous gray eyebrows were twitching, and his eyes were runny, and he looked so lost that I almost wanted to put an arm around him.

"New York! Why didn't anyone tell me?" He seemed a little confused, which is not so unusual for an older person.

"It's pretty huge in New York ever since it became *Los Pampas Casa Companeros.* They got Ricardo Dorito and Butch Tamale and Peter Ostinato and Vern Suarez and Janis Hernandez and Filipo Bracero and all the big salsa stars. It's selling out Madison Square Garden twice on Saturday plus a Sunday matinee. Busloads of college kids on Eighth Avenue. Ticket scalpers getting $150 for a seat up in the peanut gallery."

He looked at me mournfully. "I was on that show for many years."

"Yes, I know," I said.

"Believe it or not, I was the host."

"I was aware of that."

"I had a parking spot here right beside the loading dock and a dressing room of my own with a mirror and little lightbulbs all around it, and there was a production assistant who brought me coffee and cookies. I had it so good."

I asked him, "Can I call you a cab? Is there someone at home who could come and get you? Where are you living now?" He craned his neck and looked up and down the street. "My car's around here somewhere," he said. I walked him up Wabasha to Tenth Street. "I started that show in 1974," he said. "They all laughed when I told them I was going to do it, and then I got up and did my monologue, and they stopped laughing. I never missed a show. Hundred percent attendance record. Always showed up on time. I didn't want to retire, but they tricked me into taking a sabbatical, and when I returned, they had switched it to Spanish. They offered to pay for Spanish lessons, so I took those for a few months, but my teacher, Carmela, spoke a minor dialect from Yucatán that Spanish-speakers refer to as *discurso estúpido,* and when I went on the show and did a monologue in Spanish, people laughed themselves red in the face. There wasn't a dry seat in the house. I asked if I could do sound effects, and they auditioned me, and I was okay with cows, pigs, dogs, cats, primates, and tropical birds, but I couldn't whinny and my pistol shot sounded like someone coughing up marshmallows. So I took the long hike. I've been waiting for them to decide where to hold the retirement dinner. You know, where they give me the keys to a new convertible. It was supposed to be in February, but the woman who's running the show doesn't speak good English, and I think she told me the dinner will be at La Cucaracha in a couple months, which is a rather small restaurant, and that they'll present me with a bicycle." We located his car, thank God, on St. Peter. An old green Volvo with Gore 2000 bumper stickers and what looked like five hundred copies of his memoir, *A Quiet Week,* in the backseat. I noticed a credit-card stamper and a sign, AUTOGRAPHED COPIES, NO EXTRA CHARGE. The guy was driving around town selling his book out of the backseat of his car. He offered me a ride, but I said no thanks, I didn't know where I was going.

I still don't. I'm a New York guy who wound up in St. Paul, Minnesota, on the gray-green Mississippi, all for the love of a beautiful woman, and now I'm thinking maybe I'll head back to New York and find a sublet in the West Nineties and get a job with Caribbean Celebrity Sunset Cruises, whose proprietor, Smiling Max Waxman, I know from grade school. Very successful. Hires faded celebrities down on their luck and pays them peanuts and charges wealthy geezers a king's ransom to hobnob with the formerly famous, people like the Tropikettes and comedian Danny Meadows and Eddie Hobbs, who played the nosy neighbor on *That Darn Ricky,* the one with the cigar who kept saying, "What about it? What about it?" Max says he'll hire me as a Gentleman Host whose job it is to dance with unaccompanied ladies and show interest in the photos of their grandchildren. Work January through March and earn your nut for the year and, if you wish, spend April to December sitting in Central Park watching the women run past. Ah, New York. It looks mighty good to me except on even-numbered days, when I'm thinking, *Stick around. Settle down. One of these days you will meet her, and your heart will go wild and the music will play, and you'll get up and dance.* I sit in the Brew Ha Ha with my latte and work the *Times* crossword and try to look cool and unavailable yet irresistible, and inevitably some fabulous young woman plops down across the table with book in hand, and my heart goes crazy but I am cool and do not throw myself into her lap and cry out *O you you you, kiss that book goodbye, Pretty Woman, you dream maker, you four-star lover, let us dally, Little Buttercup, boop-boop-a-doop let me be your Ding Dong Daddy-O and we'll tango on our tippy-toes through Babylon, baby doll, down the Boule-*

*vard of Broken Hearts and who cares about tomorrow, baby, let them do the math, we'll have us* eine kleine amour, mio caro, *shang shang a lang, and make the bed bounce and the night get sparkly and honey drip from the stratosphere, Anything Your Heart Desires, Baby Doll, I am here to make it happen.*

No, I don't say that. I say, "How's it going?" and she says, "Okay," in a desultory way.

The Pillsbury Mill apartment is gone and that whole fantasy of elegance on the Mississippi. The checks stopped coming after Naomi sold Elongate to Larry B. Larry for a lifetime guarantee of a quarter-million per annum, and the housing bubble popped, and there I was with a monster of a mortgage. Boo-hoo for me. I gave the condo back to the bank and returned to the Shropshire Arms, tail between my legs, where Doris has mellowed somewhat and gave me a good deal on a one-bedroom one floor below my old pad, which is now occupied by a babe named Bijoux Benson, who walks barefoot across my ceiling late at night and creates beautiful visions of The Life To Come. She is a designer or something, and I've seen her only now and then, and I almost fell over from sheer admiration, the woman is long and lean and moves like a panther with a thousand-watt smile. A sweetie with brunette bedroom hair and long delicate fingers it would be a thrill just to take in my hand.

"You got a crush on her, dontcha, well la-di-da," said Doris. "You watch your step with me, or I am going to divulge to Bijoux your little secret."

"What's that?"

"You know what's that. You've got worms, mister."

*Whappppp.*

"How'd you know that, Doris?"

"A lot of people know that. So don't get on your high horse. Just do as you're told, and everything's cool."

"What are you saying, Doris?"

"I'm saying that I want you to take me out once in a while. We don't have to kiss or hold hands. I just want to maybe take your arm and sit next to you, and you can act like you're a little bit sweet on me."

Well, she had me over a barrel. Every day I listen for Bijoux unlocking her door and I dash into the hall and get on the elevator as she descends, and I get ten seconds with her, but she wouldn't smile at me so warmly if she knew I had worms, so I must now squire Doris around to a movie or concert, Doris with her croaky voice and liniment odor and sensible shoes, Doris with the big rings on her knobby fingers and the plastic bag instead of a purse.

Naomi is in Southampton with the Rama Lama Monongahela, and though she is very wealthy, she leads a simple, healthy life and has become a Positivist, which has to do with circularizing your neurons using an electric responder, which I gather plugs into an outlet implanted in your navel. I hope she is okay. She e-mails me now and then to inquire about my health and recommend particular supplements and vitamins. Sharon met a guy named Lenny Browder who roasts her beans and is good for her in other ways, I'm sure. As for me, I am still skinny, thanks to worms. I tell people it's metabolism, because if people find out you have parasites, they no longer want to sit at your table. That is a proven fact.

Sugar wanted to get back together, and maybe we could have, but one morning she called me before I'd had my second cup of coffee and said, "I called to see how you're doing."

"I'm doing okay considering that it's seven thirty a.m."

"You don't sound okay."

"Okay, why don't you tell me how I'm doing then?"

"Don't get all defensive about it."

"You call up and ask me a question, and then you answer it. It's the old story with us, Sugar. We get on the phone, and fifteen seconds later we're arguing."

"It's been more than fifteen seconds. It's been more than thirty seconds."

"Okay, forty-five seconds later we're arguing."

"I thought you'd be glad to hear from me. I didn't know you'd be timing me with a stopwatch."

I took a deep breath. "How are you, Sugar?"

"You really want to know, or you just asking to be polite?"

I told her I was asking just to be polite.

"That's what I thought. But I'll tell you anyway. Not so good."

I told her I was sorry to hear that.

"Are you really?"

I said that yes, I really was.

"I miss you so much, Guy," she said. "That's why I feel lousy. I think we've got something good between us. Why don't we go back and recapture it?"

I explained that just because we had a good time making love, it didn't mean that we were meant for each other.

This put her in a bad mood, and she talked for some time about men and their inability to commit. I did not hold the phone up close to my ear, since I had heard this talk before. I set the phone quietly on the desk, and I heard it as a pleasant distant music similar to a housefly buzzing but lovelier than that, while I busied myself paying bills. And then the buzzing stopped. I picked up the phone.

"Well?" she said.

I said, "You're absolutely right."

"So what are you going to do about it then?"

"Nothing to be done. I was in love with you once, Sugar. Once was enough. I'm immune now."

"You talk about it like it was a disease." And she hung up.

I'll bet she expected me to call her back and apologize. I didn't. So she married a Swede named Torben with a head like a pear who says dumb things in a voice you can hear a block away. Good luck with that, I say.

What did I learn from the Year of the Tapeworm? That we're all full of need, and we're not sure what for. You think you want to be skinny so you drop sixty pounds, and then you find out that what you really want is your youth, or someone to love you in that helpless, wholehearted way that is so rare in real life. As someone once said: "Give me ambiguity or give me something else." We want to be loved because we're unique, and not unique in the way that everyone is unique, but really unique. Love is what life is all about. Like all generalizations, that one is probably off the mark. But who knows? Like the song says, "Freedom's just another word for not knowing what is going on."

As for Joey Roast Beef, he is all sweetness and light, no more homicidal rages. The new meds have done wonders: a blue pill the size of a ladybug, twice a day, turned him into a genial old coot sitting in a sunny corner of Danny's with McCafferty and reminiscing about the old days at Gallivan's bar back when men smoked cigars and drank four martinis and drove home singing. A massage studio called A Touch of Wonder took over my office on the twelfth floor of the Acme Building after the Bogus Boys attack, and Lou, the manager, gave the Touch of Wonder people a six-year lease, which hurt me, what with my long tenancy, and his offer to me of a windowless cubicle in the "lower lobby" (what most people would call a *basement)* was salt in the wound, and one day I says to Joey Junior (who had heard about the worms and came to me with an idea for a fish lure with bacon for bait that is soaked in Nembutol so it numbs the fish's lips against the pain of the hook, which I told him was "interesting" but "not for me at this particular time") — I says to Joey Junior, "If a person were going to try to get the attention of a certain business, let's say, to persuade them to move and do it quicklike, not dink around for weeks and months, what might a person do? Not saying it's me or anybody I know. Just purely hypothetical."

Joey Junior sat and pondered this for a moment, all 440 pounds of him, and twiddled his jumping-walleye necktie and smoothed out the wrinkles in his green rayon suit, and he said, "Well, my hypothetical advice — not saying I'd actually recommend doing this, but strictly on a theoretical basis, just as an example of what *might* be done — I'd take a hypothetical pistol and figuratively point it at the alleged front window of the establishment and put about four to six apparent holes through the plate glass and leave an imaginary note saying, 'Next time it'll be you, dogface.' That'd be my hypotheticals on that."

"What if this business is on the twelfth floor and there are no front windows, just back windows?"

"I'd point the so-called pistol at the front door and put four to six apparent holes through that."

"Thank you for the example."

"You're very welcome."

And that very night, someone went and shot up the door of A Touch of Wonder and blasted the face cradle off their massage table and silenced the mp3 player that played the Peruvian flute music, and the massage folks found a nicer location on Grand Avenue west of Macalester College, and Lou let me back in on the condition that I fix the door myself, which I now have done.

So here I am, sitting in the swivel chair at the old oak desk next to the file cabinet, perusing Emily Dickinson's *Selected* and waiting for the knock on the door. "Success is counted sweetest by those who ne'er succeed," she wrote, and she sure got that right, pal. At night when I am listening to Bijoux upstairs as she drops her shoes on the floor and also what sounds like her jeans, and she starts running a hot shower, in my mind I am standing nearby with a big fluffy towel in hand waiting to dry her off. In fact I am waiting to accompany Doris to the Simon & Garfunkel concert at the hockey arena, and soon I must go off to the oldies, but meanwhile I am standing beside the glass door all steamed up (the door, that is) through which I watch the beautiful Bijoux move like the dreamboat spirit of all the women I spent my dreams on, all the magnificent ladies, I don't regret a single night I spent with any of them.

# ABOUT THE AUTHOR

**Garrison Keillor** created Guy Noir in 1994 as a recurring segment on *A Prairie Home Companion,* playing Guy himself with Walter Bobbie as Pete and later Tim Russell as McCafferty, Jimmy, Rico, and other roles; Sue Scott as Sugar and Doris; and Tom Keith as Wendell and Joey.

Keillor grew up in Minnesota listening to *Dragnet* and *The Shadow* on the radio, and worked his way through the University of Minnesota as a radio announcer. He lives in St. Paul and New York.